The Djinn in
the Nightingale's Eye

The Djinn in
the Nightingale's Eye

FIVE FAIRY STORIES

A. S. BYATT

A S Byatt

Chatto & Windus

LONDON

First published in Great Britain 1994

3 5 7 9 10 8 6 4 2

© A. S. Byatt 1994

Published in 1994 by
Chatto & Windus Limited
Random House, 20 Vauxhall Bridge Road
London SWIV 2SA

Random House Australia (Pty) Limited
20 Alfred Street, Milsons Point, Sydney
New South Wales 2061, Australia

Random House New Zealand Limited
18 Poland Road, Glenfield
Auckland 10, New Zealand

Random House South Africa (Pty) Limited
PO Box 337, Bergvlei, South Africa

Random House UK Limited Reg. No. 954009

A CIP catalogue record for this book
is available from the British Library

ISBN 07011 6278 3

Designed by Humphrey Stone
Photoset in Fournier by SX Composing Ltd, Rayleigh, Essex
Printed in Great Britain by Clays Ltd, St Ives plc

For Cevat Çapan

Contents

The Glass Coffin

The Crystal Coffin, H.J. Ford, 1892

The Glass Coffin

There was once a little tailor, a good and unre-
markable man, who happened to be journeying
through a forest, in search of work perhaps, for in
those days men travelled great distances to make a
meagre living, and the services of a fine craftsman,
like our hero, were less in demand than cheap and
cobbling hasty work that fitted ill and lasted only
briefly. He believed he should come across someone who would want his skills – he was an
incurable optimist, and imagined a fortunate meeting around every corner, though how that should
come about was hard to see, as he advanced farther
and farther into the dark, dense trees, where even
the moonlight was split into dull little needles of
bluish light on the moss, not enough to see by. But
he did come upon the little house that was waiting
for him, in a clearing in the depths, and was cheered
by the lines of yellow light he could see between
and under the shutters. He knocked boldly on the

door of this house, and there was a rustling, and creaking, and the door opened a tiny crack, and there stood a little man, with a face as grey as morning ashes, and a long woolly beard the same colour.

'I am a traveller lost in the woods,' said the little tailor, 'and a master craftsman, seeking work, if any is to be found.'

'I have no need for a master craftsman,' said the little grey man. 'And I am afraid of thieves. You cannot come in here.'

'If I were a thief I could have forced my way in, or crept secretly in,' said the little tailor. 'I am an honest tailor in need of help.'

Now behind the little man stood a great grey dog, as tall as he was, with red eyes and hot breath. And at first this beast had made a low girning, growling sound, but now he hushed his threatening, and waved his tail slowly, and the little grey man said, 'Otto is of the opinion that you are honest. You may have a bed for the night in return for an honest evening's work, for help with cooking and cleaning and what must be prepared in my simple home.'

So the tailor was let in, and there was a strange household. In a rocking chair stood a brilliantly coloured cockerel and his pure white wife. In the fire-corner stood a black-and-white goat, with knobby little horns and eyes like yellow glass, and on the hearth lay a very large cat, a multi-coloured, mazy-patterned brindled cat, that looked up at the little tailor with eyes like cold green jewels, with black slits for pupils. And behind the dining table was a delicate dun cow, with milky breath and a warm wet nose and enormous soft brown eyes. 'Good morning,' said the tailor to this company, for he believed in good manners, and the creatures were surveying him in a judging and intelligent way.

'Food and drink you will find in the kitchen,' said the little grey man. 'Make us a fit supper and we will eat together.'

So the little tailor turned to, and prepared a splendid pie, from flour and meat and onions he found there, and decorated its top with beautifully formed pastry leaves and flowers, for he was a craftsman, even if he could not exercise his own craft. And whilst it was cooking he looked about him, and brought hay to the cow and goat, golden corn to the cock and hen, milk to the cat and bones and meat from his cooking to the great grey dog. And when the tailor and the little grey man were consuming the pie, whose warm smell filled the little house, the little grey man said, 'Otto was right, you are a good and honest man, and you care for all the creatures in this place, leaving no one un-attended and nothing undone. I shall give you a gift for your kindness. Which of these things will you have?'

And he laid before the tailor three things. The first was a little purse of soft leather, which clinked a little as he put it down. The second was a cooking pot, black outside, polished and gleaming inside, solid and commodious. And the third was a little glass key, wrought into a fantastic fragile shape, and glittering with all the colours of the rainbow. And the tailor looked at the watching animals for advice, and they all stared benignly back. And he thought to himself, I know about such gifts from forest people. It may be that the first is a purse which is never empty, and the second a pot which provides a wholesome meal whenever you demand

6

one in the right way. I have heard of such things and met men who have been paid from such purses and eaten from such pots. But a glass key I never saw or heard of and cannot imagine what use it might be; it would shiver in any lock. But he desired the little glass key, because he was a craftsman, and could see that it had taken masterly skill to blow all these delicate wards and barrel, and because he did not have any idea about what it was or might do, and curiosity is a great power in men's lives. So he said to the little man, 'I will take the pretty glass key.' And the little man answered, 'You have chosen not with prudence, but with daring. The key is the key to an adventure, if you will go in search of it.'

'Why not?' replied the tailor. 'Since there is no use for my craft in this wild place, and since I have not chosen prudently.'

Then the animals came closer with their warm, milky breaths that smelled sweetly of hay and the summer, and their mild comforting gaze that was not human, and the dog lay with his heavy head on the tailor's foot, and the brindled cat sat on the arm of his chair.

'You must go out of this house,' said the little grey man, 'and call to the West Wind, and show her your key, when she comes, and let her carry you where she will, without struggle or alarm. If you fight or question she will toss you on the thorns and it will go ill with you before you come out of there. If she will take you, you will be set down in a bare heath, on a great stone, which is made of granite and is the gate to your adventure, though it will seem to have been fixed and un-moving since the making of the world. On this stone you must lay a feather from the tail of the cockerel here, which he will willingly give you, and the door will be opened to you. You must descend without fear, or hesitation, and descend further, and still descend; you will find that your glass key will shed light on your way if you hold it before you. In time you will come to a stone vestibule, with two doors leading to branching passages you must not follow, and a low curtained door leading on and downwards. You must not touch this cur-tain with your hand, but must lay on it the milk-white feather which the hen will give you, and the curtain will be opened silently, by unseen

8

hands, and the doors beyond it will lie open, and you may come into the hall where you shall find what you shall find.'

'Well, I will adventure,' said the little tailor, 'though I have great fear of the dark places under the earth, where there is no light of day and what is above is dense and heavy.' So the cock and the hen allowed him to take a glistening burnished black and emerald feather and a soft creamy-white feather, and he bade them all goodbye and went into the clearing, and called to the West Wind, holding up his key.

And that was a delightful and most alarming sensation, when the long, airy arms of the West Wind reached down through the trees and caught him up, and the leaves were all shivering and clattering and trembling with her passing, and the straws danced before the house and the dust rose and flew about in little earth-fountains. The trees grabbed at him with twiggy fingers as he rose up through them, lurching this way and that in the gusts, and then he felt himself held against the invisible rushing breast of the long Wind, as she hurled moaning along the sky. He rested his face

9

against his airy pillows, and did not cry out or struggle, and the sighing song of the West Wind, full of fine rain and glancing sunshine, streaming clouds and driven starlight, netted him around and around.

She put him down as the little grey man had foretold on a huge grey granite stone, pitted and scarred and bald. He heard her whisking and wailing on her way, and he bent down and laid the cock-feather on the stone, and behold with a heavy groaning and grinding the huge stone swung up in the air and down in the earth, as though on a pivot or balance, disturbing waves of soil and heather like thick sea-water, and showing a dark, dank passage under the heather-roots and the knotty roots of the gorse. So in he went, bravely enough, thinking all the time of the thickness of rock and peat and earth over his head, and the air in that place was chill and damp and the ground underfoot was moist and sodden. He bethought him of his little key and held it up bravely before him, and it put out a little sparkling light that illumined a step at a time, silvery-pale. So he came down to the vestibule, where the three doors were, and under the sills of the two great doors light shone, warm and enticing, and the third was behind a musty leather curtain. He touched this leather, just brushing it with the tip of his soft hen-feather, and it was drawn away in angular folds like bat-wings, and beyond a little dark door lay open into a tiny hole, into which he thought he might just manage to put his shoulders. Then truly he was afraid, for his small grey friend had said nothing of this narrow little place, and he thought if he put his head in he might never come out alive.

So he looked behind himself and saw that the passage he had just come down was one of many, all wrinkled and wormy and dripping and tangled with roots, and he thought he could never find his way back so he must perforce push on and see what lay in store. It took all the courage he had to thrust his head and shoulders into the mouth of that entrance, but he closed his eyes and twisted and turned and after a time tumbled out into a great stone chamber, lit with a soft light of its own that dimmed the glitter of his shining key. It was a miracle, he thought, that the glass had not shivered in that tight struggle, but it was as clear and brittle as ever. So he looked about him, and saw three things. The first was a heap of glass bottles and flasks, all of them covered with dust and cobwebs. The second was a glass dome, the size of a man, and a little taller than our hero. And the third was a shining glass coffin, lying on a rich velvet pall on a gilded trestle. And from all these things the soft light proceeded, like the glimmering of pearls in the depth of water, like the phosphorescent light that moves of itself on the night surface of southern seas, or shines round the heaving shoals, milky-white over their silver darts, in our own dark Channel.

Well, he thought, one or all of these is my adventure. He looked at the bottles, which were many colours, red and green and blue and smoky topaz, and contained wisps and rinsings of nothing much, a sigh of smoke in one, a rocking of spirituous liquid in another. All were corked and sealed, and he was too circumspect to break the seals till he saw better where he was and what was to do.

He moved on to the dome, which you must imagine like the magic covers you have seen in your drawing-room under which dwell all sorts of brilliant little birds, as natural as life on their branches, or flights of mysterious moths and butterflies. Or maybe you have seen a crystal ball containing a tiny house which you can shake to produce a brilliant snowstorm? This dome contained a whole castle, set in a beautiful park, with trees and terraces and gardens, fishpools and climbing roses, and bright banners hanging limp in its many turrets. It was a brave and beautiful place, with innumerable windows and twisting staircases and a lawn and a swing in a tree and everything you could desire in a spacious and desirable residence, only that it was all still and tiny enough to need a magnifying glass to see the intricacies of its carvings and appurtenances. The little tailor, as I have told you, was first and foremost a craftsman, and he stared in wonder at this beautiful model and could not begin to imagine what fine tools or instruments had carved and wrought it. He dusted it a little, to marvel better, and then moved on to the glass coffin.

Have you remarked, where a fast-flowing stream comes to a little fall, how the racing water becomes glassy smooth and under it the long fine threads of the water-weed are drawn along in its still-seeming race, trembling a little, but stretched out in the flow? So under the surface of the thick glass lay a mass of long gold threads, filling in the whole cavity of the box with their turns and tumbles, so that at first the little tailor thought he had come upon a box full of spun gold, to make cloth of gold. But then between the fronds he saw a face, the most beautiful face he could have dreamed of or imagined, a still white face, with long gold lashes on pale cheeks, and a perfect pale mouth. Her gold hair lay round her like a mantle, but where its strands crossed her face they stirred a little with her breathing, so that the tailor knew she was alive. And he knew – it is always so, after all – that the true adventure was the release of this sleeper, who would then be his grateful bride. But she was so beautiful and peaceful that he was half-loath to disturb her. He wondered how she had come there, and how long she had been there, and what her voice would be like, and a thousand other ridiculous things, whilst she breathed in and out, ruffling the gold threads of hair.

And then he saw, in the side of the smooth box,

which had no visible cleft or split, but was whole like a green ice egg, a tiny keyhole. And he knew that this was the keyhole for his wondrous delicate key, and with a little sigh he put it in and waited for what should ensue. As the little key slipped into the keyhole and melted, as it seemed into the glass body of the casket, so for a moment the whole surface was perfectly closed and smooth. And then, in a very orderly way, and with a strange bell-like tinkling, the coffin broke into a collection of long icicle splinters, that rang and vanished as they touched the earth. And the sleeper opened her eyes, which were as blue as periwinkle, or the summer sky, and the little tailor, because he knew this was what he must do, bent and kissed the perfect cheek.

'You must be the one,' said the young woman, 'you must be the one I have been waiting for, who must release me from enchantment. You must be the Prince.'

'Ah no,' said our hero, 'there you are mistaken. I am no more – and indeed no less – than a fine craftsman, a tailor, in search of work for my hands, honest work, to keep me alive.'

Then the young woman laughed merrily, her voice strengthening after what must have been years of silence, and the whole strange cellar rang with that laughter, and the glass fragments tinkled like broken bells.

'You shall have enough and more than enough, to keep you alive forever, if you help me out of this dark place,' she said. 'Do you see that beautiful castle locked in glass?'

'Indeed I do, and marvel at the craft with which it was made.'

'That was no carver's or miniaturist's craft, but black magic, for that was the castle in which I lived, and the forests and meadows round it were mine, where I roamed freely, with my beloved brother, until the black artist came one night seeking shelter from foul weather. For you must know that I had a twin brother, as beautiful as the day, and gentle as a fawn, and wholesome as new bread and butter, whose company pleased me so much, as mine also pleased him, that we swore an oath never to marry but to live forever peacefully in the castle, and hunt and play together the livelong day. But when this stranger knocked, in a howling gale, with his wet hat and cloak pouring rainwater and his smiling mouth, my brother invited him in eagerly, and gave him meat and wine, and a bed for the night, and sang with him, and played cards, and sat by the fire, talking of the wide world and its adventures. As I was not pleased with this, and indeed a little sorrowful that my brother should take pleasure in another's company, I went to bed early and lay listening to the West Wind howling round the turrets and after a while fell into an uneasy slumber. From this I was wakened by a strange, very beautiful twanging music, coming from all about me. I sat up, and tried to see what this might be or mean, and saw the door of my chamber slowly open and he, the stranger, came striding in, dry now, with black curly hair and a dangerous smiling face. I tried to move, but could not, it was as though a band gripped my body, and another band was tied about my face. He told me that he meant me no harm, but was a magician, who had made the music play around me, and wished to have my hand in marriage and live in my castle, with me and my brother, in peace hereafter. And I said – for I was permitted to answer – that I had no desire for marriage, but wished to live unwed and happy with my dear brother and no other. So he answered that that might not be, that he would have me whether I would or no, and that my brother was of his opinion in this matter. We shall see that, said I, and he answered unabashed, with the invisible instruments twanging and humming and jangling all over the room, "You may see it, but you must not speak about this or anything that has passed here, for I have silenced you as surely as if I had cut out your tongue."

'Next day I tried to warn my brother, and it was as the black artist had said. When I opened my mouth to speak on this topic it was as though my lips were sewn together with great stitches in the flesh, and my tongue would not move in my mouth. Yet I might ask to have the salt passed, or discourse of the evil weather, and so my brother, to my great chagrin, noticed nothing, but set out blithely to go hunting with his new friend, leaving me at home to sit by the hearth, and to feel silent anguish at what might ensue. All day I sat so, and in the late afternoon, when the shadows were long on the castle lawns and the last rays of the sun were brassy and chill, I knew with certainty that something terrible had happened, and ran out of the castle, and away to the dark woods. And out of the dark woods came the black man, leading his horse on one arm, and on the other a tall grey hound with the saddest face I have ever seen on any creature. He told me my brother had suddenly gone away, and would return no more for a great and uncertain length of time and had left me, and the castle, in charge of him, the dark magician. He told me this gaily, as if it did not much matter whether I believed it or no. I said I would by no means submit to such injustice and was glad to hear my own voice steady and confident, for I feared my lips might again be sewn into silence. When I spoke great tears fell from the eyes of the grey hound, more and more, heavier and heavier. And I knew in some sort, I think, that the animal was my brother, in this meek and helpless form. Then I was angry, and said he should never come into my house, nor come near me, with my good will. And he said that I had perceived correctly, that he might do nothing without my good will which he would strive to gain, if I would allow it. And I said, this should never be, and he must never hope for it. Then he became angry, and threatened that he would silence me forever, if I would not agree. I said that without my dear brother I had little care where I was, and no one I wished to speak to. Then he said I should see whether that was so after a hundred years in a glass coffin. He made a few passes and the castle diminished and shrank, as you see it now, and he made a pass or two more and it was walled with glass as you see. And my people, the men and maidservants who came running, he confined as you see, each in a glass bottle, and finally closed me into the glass coffin in which you found me. And now, if you will have me, we will hasten from this place, before the magician returns, as he does from time to time, to see if I have relented.'

'Of course I will have you,' said the little tailor, 'for you are my promised marvel, released with my vanished glass key, and I love you dearly already. Though why you should have me, simply because I opened the glass case, is less clear to me alto-gether, and when, and if, you are restored to your rightful place, and your home and lands and people are again your own, I trust you will feel free to re-consider the matter, and remain, if you will, alone and unwed. For me, it is enough to have seen the extraordinary gold web of your hair, and to have touched that whitest and most delicate cheek with my lips.' And you may ask yourselves, my dear and most innocent readers, whether he spoke there with more gentleness or cunning, since the lady set such store on giving herself of her own free will, and since also the castle with its gardens, though now measurable with pins and fine stitches and thumbnails and thimbles, were lordly and hand-some enough for any man to wish to spend his days there. The beautiful lady then blushed, a warm and rosy colour in her white cheeks, and was heard to murmur that the spell was as the spell was, that a kiss received after the successful disintegration of the glass casket was a promise, as kisses are, whether received voluntarily or involuntarily. Whilst they were thus disputing, politely, the moral niceties of their interesting situation, a rush-ing sound was heard, and a melodious twanging, and the lady became very agitated, and said the black magician was on his way. And our hero, in his turn, felt despondent and fearful, for his little grey mentor had given him no instructions for this eventuality. Still, he thought, I must do what I can to protect the lady, to whom I owe so much, and whom I have certainly, for better, for worse, released from sleep and silence. He carried no weapon save his own sharp needles and scissors, but it occurred to him that he could make do with the slivers of glass from the broken sarcophagus. So he took up the longest and sharpest, wrapping its hilt round in his leather apron, and waited.

The black artist appeared on the threshold, wrapped in a swirling black cloak, smiling most ferociously, and the little tailor quaked and held up his splinter, thinking his foe would be bound to meet it magically, or freeze his hand in motion as he struck. But the other merely advanced, and when he came up, put out a hand to touch the lady, whereupon our hero struck with all his might at his heart, and the glass splinter entered deeply and he fell to the ground. And behold, he shrivelled and withered under their eyes, and became a small handful of grey dust and glass powder. Then the lady wept a little, and said that the tailor had now

twice saved her, and was in every way worthy of
her hand. And she clapped her hands together, and
suddenly they all rose in the air, man, woman,
house, glass flasks, heap of dust, and found themselves out on a cold hillside where stood the
original little grey man with Otto the hound. And
you, my sagacious readers, will have perceived and
understood that Otto was the very same hound
into which the young brother of the lady of the coffin had been transformed. So she fell upon his grey
hairy neck, weeping bright tears. And when her
tears mixed with the salty tears that fell down the
great beasts's cheek, the spell was released, and he
stood before her, a golden-haired young man in
hunting-costume. And they embraced, for a long
time, with full hearts. Meanwhile the little tailor,
aided by the little grey man, had stroked the glass
case containing the castle with the two feathers
from the cock and hen, and with a strange rushing
and rumbling the castle appeared as it must always
have been, with noble staircases and innumerable
doors. Then the little tailor and the little grey man
uncorked the bottles and flasks and the liquids and
smokes flowed sighing out of the necks of them,

and formed themselves into men and women, butler and forester, cook and parlourmaid, all mightily bewildered to find themselves where they were. Then the lady told her brother that the little tailor had rescued her from her sleep and had killed the black artist and had won her hand in marriage. And the young man said that the tailor had offered him kindness, and should live with them both in the castle and be happy ever after. And so it was, and they did live happily ever after. The young man and his sister went hunting in the wild woods, and the little tailor, whose inclination did not lie that way, stayed by the hearth and was merry with them in the evenings. Only one thing was missing. A craftsman is nothing without the exercise of his craft. So he ordered to be brought to him the finest silk cloth and brilliant threads, and made for pleasure what he had once needed to make for harsh necessity.

Gode's Story

En pleine mer, René Quillivic, born 1879

Gode's Story

There was once a young sailor who had nothing but his courage and his bright eyes – but those were *very* bright – and the strength the gods gave him, which was sufficient.

He was not a good match for any girl in the village, for he was thought to be rash as well as poor, but the young girls liked to see him go by, you can believe, and they liked most particularly to see him dance, with his long, long legs and his clever feet and his laughing mouth.

And most of all one girl liked to see him, who was the miller's daughter, beautiful and stately and proud, with three deep velvet ribbons to her skirt, who would by no means let him see that she liked to see him, but looked sideways with glimpy eyes, when he was not watching. And so did many another. It is always so. Some are looked at, and some may whistle for an admiring glance till the devil pounces on them, for so the Holy Spirit makes, crooked or straight, and naught to be done about it.

He came and went, the young man, for it was the long voyages he was drawn to, he went with the whales over the edge of the world and down to where the sea boils and the great fish move under it like drowned islands and the mermaids sing with their mirrors and their green scales and their winding hair, if tales are to be believed. He was first up the mast and sharpest with the harpoon but he made no money, for the profit was all the master's, and so he came and went.

And when he came he sat in the square and told of what he had seen, and they all listened. And the miller's daughter came, all clean and proud and proper, and he saw her listening at the edge and said he would bring her a silk ribbon from the East, if she liked. And she would not say if she liked, yes or no, but he saw that she would.

And he went again, and had the ribbon from a silk-merchant's daughter in one of those countries where the women are golden with hair like black silk, but they like to see a man dance with long, long legs, and clever feet and a laughing mouth.

And he told the silk-merchant's daughter he would come again and brought back the ribbon, all laid up in a perfumed paper, and at the next village dance he gave it to the miller's daughter and said, 'Here is your ribbon.'

And her heart banged in her side, you may believe, but she mastered it, and asked coolly how much she was to pay him for it. It was a lovely ribbon, a rainbow-coloured silk ribbon, such as had never been seen in these parts.

And he was very angry at this insult to his gift, and said she must pay what it had cost her from whom he had it. And she said,

'What was that?'

And he said, 'Sleepless nights till I come again.'

And she said, 'The price is too high.'

And he said, 'The price is set, you must pay.'

And she paid, you may believe, for he saw how it was with her, and a man hurt in his pride will take what he may, and he took, for she had seen him dance, and she was all twisted and turned in her mind and herself by his pride and his dancing.

And he said, if he went away again, and found

some future in any part of the world, would she wait till he came again and asked her father for her.

And she said, 'Long must I wait, and you with a woman waiting in every port, and a ribbon fluttering in every breeze on every quay, if I wait for you.'

And he said, 'You will wait.'

And she would not say yes or no, she would wait or not wait.

And he said, 'You are a woman with a cursed temper, but I will come again and you will see.'

And after a time, the people saw that her beauty dimmed, and her step grew creeping, and she did not lift her head, and she grew heavy all over. And she took to waiting in the harbour, to see the ships come in, and though she asked after none, everyone knew well enough why she was there, and who it was she waited for. But she said nothing to anyone. Only she was seen up on the point, where the Lady Chapel is, praying, it must be thought, though none heard her prayers.

And after more time, when many ships had come and gone, and others had been wrecked, and their men swallowed, but his had not been seen or heard of, the miller thought he heard an owl cry, or a cat miawl in his barn, but when he came there was no one and nothing, only blood on the straw. So he called his daughter and she came, deathly-white, rubbing her eyes as if in sleep, and he said, 'Here is blood on the straw,' and she said, 'I would thank you not to wake me from my good sleep to tell me the dog has killed a rat, or the cat eaten a mouse here in the barn.'

And they all saw she was white, but she stood upright, holding her candle, and they all went in again.

And then the ship came home, over the line of sea and into the harbour, and the young man leaped to the shore to see if she was waiting, and she was not. Now he had seen her in his mind's eye, all round the globe, as clear as clear, waiting there, with her proud pretty face, and the coloured ribbon in the breeze, and his heart hardened, you will understand, that she had not come. But he did not ask after her, only kissed the girls and smiled and ran up the hill to his house.

And by and by he saw a pale thin thing creeping along in the shadow of a wall, all slow and halting. And he did not know her at first. And she thought to creep past him like that, because she was so altered.

He said, 'You did not come.'

And she said, 'I could not.'

And he said, 'You are here in the street all the same.'

And she said, 'I am not what I was.'

And he said, 'What is that to me? But you did not come.'

And she said, 'If it is nothing to you, it is much to me. Time has passed. What is past is past. I must go.'

And she did go.

And that night he danced with Jeanne, the smith's daughter, who had fine white teeth and little plump hands like fat rosebuds.

And the next day he went to seek the miller's daughter and found her in the chapel on the hill.

He said, 'Come down with me.'

And she said, 'Do you hear little feet, little bare feet, dancing?'

And he said, 'No, I hear the sea on the shore, and the air running over the dry grass, and the weather-cock grinding round in the wind.'

And she said, 'All night they danced in my head, round this way and back that, so that I did not sleep.'

And he, 'Come down with me.'

And she, 'But can you not hear the dancer?'

And so it went on for a week or a month, or two months, he dancing with Jeanne, and going up to the chapel and getting only the one answer from the miller's daughter, and in the end he wearied, as rash and handsome men will, and said, 'I have waited as you would not, come now, or I shall wait no more.'

And she, 'How can I come if you cannot hear the little thing dancing?'

And he said, 'Stay with your little thing then, if you love it better than me.'

And she said not a word, but listened to the sea and the air and the weathercock, and he left her.

And he married Jeanne the smith's daughter, and there was much dancing at the wedding, and the piper played, you may believe, and the drums hopped and rolled, and he skipped high with his long long legs and his clever feet and his laughing mouth and Jeanne was quite red with whirling and twirling, and outside the wind got up and the clouds swallowed the stars. But they went to bed in good spirits enough, full of good cider, and closed their bed-doors against the weather and were snug and tumbled in feathers.

And the miller's daughter came out in the street in her shift and bare feet, running this way and that, holding out her hands like a woman running after a strayed hen, calling 'Wait a little, wait a little.' And *some* claimed to have seen a tiny naked child dancing and prancing in front of her, round this way, back widdershins, signing with little pointy fingers and with its hair like a little mop of yellow fire. And *some* said there was nothing but a bit of blown dust whirling in the road, with a hair or two and a twig caught in it. And the miller's apprentice said he had heard little naked feet patting and slip-slapping in the loft for weeks before. And the old wives and the bright young men who know no better, said he had heard mice. But he said he had heard enough mice in his lifetime to know what was and was not mice, and he was generally credited with good sense.

So the miller's daughter ran after the dancing thing, on through the streets and the square and up

the hill to the chapel, tearing her shins on the brambles and always holding out her hands and calling
out 'Wait, oh wait.' But the thing danced on and on,
it was full of life, you may believe, it glittered and
twisted and turned and stamped its tiny feet on the
pebbles and the turf, and she struggled with the
wind in her skirts and the dark in her face. And over
the cliff went she, calling 'Wait, wait,' and so fell to
her death on the needle-rocks below and they got
her back at low tide, all bruised and broken, no
beautiful sight at all, as you may understand.

But when he came out into the street and saw it,
he took her hand and said, 'This is because I had no
faith and would not believe in your little dancing
thing. But now I hear it, plain as plain.'

And poor Jeanne had no joy of him from that
day.

And when Toussaint came he woke in his bed
with a start and heard little hands that tapped, and
little feet that stamped, all round the four sides of
his bed, and shrill little voices calling in tongues he
knew not, though he had travelled the globe.

So he threw off the covers, and looked out, and
there was the little thing, naked, and blue with cold

yet rosy with heat so it seemed to him, like a sea
fish and a summer flower, and it tossed its fiery
head and danced away and he came after. And he
came after and he came after, as far as the Baie des
Trépassés and the night was clear but there was a
veil of mist over the bay.

And the long lines of the waves came in from the
Ocean, one after another after another, and always
another, and he could see the Dead, riding the
crests of them, coming in from another world, thin
and grey and holding out helpless arms, and toss-
ing and calling in their high voices. And the
dancing thing stamped and tossed on and on, and
he came to a boat with its prow to the sea, and
when he came into the boat he felt it was full of
moving forms pressed closely together, brimming
over but unseen.

He said there were so many Dead, in the boat, on
the crests of the waves, that he felt a panic of terror
for being so crowded. For though they were all in-
substantial so he could put his hand this way or
that, yet they packed around him, and shrilled their
wild cries on the waves, so many, so many, as
though the wake of a ship would have not a flock of

36

gulls calling after it, but the sky and the sea solid with feathers, and every feather a soul, so it was he said, after.

And he said to the dancing child, 'Shall we put to sea in this boat?'

And the thing was still and would not answer.

And he said, 'So far I have come, and I am very greatly afraid, but if I may come to her, I will go on.'

And the little thing said, 'Wait.'

And he thought of her among all the others out on the water, with her thin white face and her flat breast and her starved mouth, and he called after her 'Wait,' and her voice howled back like an echo, 'Wait.'

And he stirred the air, that was full of things, with his arms, and shuffled his clever feet among the dust of the dead on the boards of that boat, but all was heavy, and would not move, and the waves went rolling past, one after another, after another, after another. Then he tried to jump in, he says, but could not. So he stood till dawn and felt them come and go and well in and draw back and heard their cries and the little thing that said,

'Wait.'

And in the dawn of the next day he came back to the village a broken man. And he sat in the square with the old men, he in the best of his manhood, and his mouth slackened and his face fell away and mostly he said nothing, except 'I can hear well enough' or otherwise 'I wait,' these two things only.

And two or three or ten years ago he put up his head and said, 'Do you not hear the little thing, dancing?' And they said no, but he went in, and made his bed businesslike, and called his neighbours and gave Jeanne the key to his sea-chest and stretched himself out, all thin as he was and wasted, and said, 'In the end I waited longest, but now I hear it stamping, the little thing is impatient, though I have been patient enough.' And at midnight he said, 'Why, there you are, then,' and so he died.

And the room smelled of apple blossom and ripe apples together, Jeanne said. And Jeanne married the butcher and bore him four sons and two daughters, all of them lusty, but ill-disposed for dancing.

The Story of the Eldest Princess

The Lady with the Rooks, Edward Calvert, 1829

The Story of the Eldest Princess

Once upon a time, in a kingdom between the sea and the mountains, between the forest and the desert, there lived a King and Queen with three daughters. Their eldest daughter was pale and quiet, the second daughter was brown and active, and the third was one of those Sabbath daughters who are bonny and bright and good and gay, of whom everything and nothing was expected.

When the eldest Princess was born, the sky was a speedwell blue, covered with very large, lazy, sheep-curly white clouds. When the second Princess was born, there were grey and creamy mares' tails streaming at great speed across the blue. And when the third Princess was born, the sky was a perfectly clear pane of sky-blue, with not a cloud to be seen, so that you might think the blue was spangled with sun-gold, though this was an illusion.

By the time they were young women, things had changed greatly. When they were infants, there were a series of stormy sunsets tinged with sea-green, and seaweed-green. Later there were, as well as the sunsets, dawns, where the sky was mackerel-puckered and underwater-dappled with lime-green and bottle-green and other greens too, malachite and jade. And when they were moody girls the green colours flecked and streaked the blue and the grey all day long, ranging from bronze-greens through emerald to palest opal-greens, with hints of fire. In the early days the people stood in the streets and fields with their mouths open, and said oh, and ah, in tones of admiration and wonder. Then one day a small girl said to her mother that there had been no blue at all for three days now, and she wanted to see blue again. And her mother told her to be sensible and patient and it would blow over, and in about a month the sky was blue, or mostly blue, but only for few days, and streaked, ominously, the people now felt, with aquamarine. And the blue days were further and further apart, and the greens were more and more varied, until a time when it became quite clear that the fundamental colour of the sky was no longer what they still called sky-blue, but a new sky-green, a pale flat green somewhere between the colours which had once been apple and grass and fern. But of course apple and grass and fern looked very different against this new light, and something very odd and dimming happened to lemons and oranges, and something more savage and hectic to poppies and pomegranates and ripe chillies.

The people, who had at first been entranced, became restive, and, as people will, blamed the King and Queen for the disappearance of the blue sky. They sent deputations to ask for its return, and they met and muttered in angry knots in the Palace Square. The royal couple consulted each other, and assured each other that they were blameless of greening, but they were uneasy, as it is deep in human nature to suppose human beings, oneself or others, to be responsible for whatever happens. So they consulted the chief ministers, the priests, and a representative sample of generals, witches and wizards. The ministers said nothing could be done, though a contingency-fund might usefully be set up for when a course of action became clear. The priests counselled patience and self-denial, as a general sanative measure, abstention from lentils, and the consumption of more lettuce. The generals supposed it might help to attack their neighbour to the East, since it was useful to have someone else to blame, and the marches and battles would distract the people.

The witches and wizards on the whole favoured a Quest. One rather powerful and generally taciturn wizard, who had interfered very little, but always successfully, in affairs of State, came out of his cavern, and said that someone must be sent along the Road through the Forest across the Desert and into the Mountains, to fetch back the single silver bird and her nest of ash-branches. The bird, he added, was kept in the walled garden of the Old Man of the Mountains, where she sipped from the crystal fountain of life, and was guarded by a thicket of thorns – poisonous thorns – and an interlaced ring of venomous fiery snakes. He believed that advice could be sought along the way about how to elude their vigilance, but the only advice he could give was to keep to the Road, and stray neither in the Forest, nor in the Desert, nor in the rocky paths, and always to be courteous. Then he went back to his cavern.

The King and Queen called together the Council of State, which consisted of themselves, their daughters, the chief minister and an old duchess, to decide what to do. The minister advised the Quest, since that was a positive action, which would please the people, and not disrupt the state. The second Princess said she would go of course, and the old duchess went to sleep. The King said he thought it should be done in an orderly manner, and he rather believed that the eldest Princess should go, since she was the first, and could best remember the blue sky. Quite why that mattered so much, no one knew, but it seemed to, and the eldest Princess said she was quite happy to set out that day, if that was what the council believed was the right thing to do.

So she set out. They gave her a sword, and an inexhaustible water-bottle someone had brought back from another Quest, and a package of bread and quails' eggs and lettuce and pomegranates, which did not last very long. They all gathered at the city gate to wish her well, and a trumpeter blew a clear, silver sound into the emptiness ahead, and a minister produced a map of the Road, with one or two sketchy patches, especially in the Desert, where its undeviating track tended to be swallowed by sandstorms.

The eldest Princess travelled quickly enough along the Road. Once or twice she thought she saw an old woman ahead of her, but this figure vanished at certain bends and slopes of the path, and did not reappear for some time, and then only briefly, so that it was never clear to the Princess whether there was one, or a succession of old women. In any case, if they were indeed, or she was indeed, an old woman, or old women, she or they were always very far ahead, and travelling extremely fast.

The Forest stretched along the Road. Pale green glades along its edges, deeper rides, and dark tangled patches beyond these. The Princess could hear, but not see, birds calling and clattering and croaking in the trees. And occasional butterflies sailed briefly out of the glades towards the Road, busy small scarlet ones, lazily swooping midnight-blue ones, and once, a hand-sized transparent one, a shimmering film of wings with two golden eyes in the centre of the lower wing. This creature hovered over the Road, and seemed to follow the Princess for several minutes, but without ever crossing some invisible barrier between Forest and Road. When it dipped and turned back into the dappled light of the trees the Princess wanted to go after it, to walk on the grass and moss, and knew she must not. She felt a little hungry by now, although she had the inexhaustible water-bottle.

She began to think. She was by nature a reading, not a travelling princess. This meant both that she enjoyed her new striding solitude in the fresh air, and that she had read a great many stories in her spare time, including several stories about princes and princesses who set out on Quests. What they all had in common, she thought to herself, was a pattern in which the two elder sisters, or brothers, set out very confidently, failed in one way or another, and were turned to stone, or imprisoned in vaults, or cast into magic sleep, until rescued by the third royal person, who did everything well, restored the first and the second, and fulfilled the Quest.

She thought she would not like to waste seven

years of her brief life as a statue or prisoner if it could be avoided.

She thought that of course she could be vigilant, and very courteous to all passers-by – most elder princesses' failings were failings of courtesy or over-confidence.

There was nobody on the Road to whom she could be courteous, except the old woman, or women, bundling along from time to time a long way ahead.

She thought, I am in a pattern I know, and I suspect I have no power to break it, and I am going to meet a test and fail it, and spend seven years as a stone.

This distressed her so much that she sat down on a convenient large stone at the side of the road and began to weep.

The stone seemed to speak to her in a thin, creaking, dry sort of voice. 'Let me out,' it said. 'I cannot get out.' It sounded irritable and angry.

The Princess jumped up. 'Who are you?' she cried. 'Where are you?'

'I am trapped under this stone,' buzzed the voice. 'I cannot get out. Roll away the stone.'

The Princess put her hands gingerly to the stone and pushed. Pinned underneath it, in a hollow of the ground was a very large and dusty scorpion, waving angry pincers, and somewhat crushed in the tail.

'Did you speak?'

'Indeed I did. I was screaming. It took you an age to hear me. Your predecessor on this Road sat down just here rather heavily when I was cooling myself in this good crack, and pinched my tail, as you see.'

'I am glad to have been able to help,' said the Princess, keeping a safe distance.

The Scorpion did not answer, as it was trying to raise itself and move forwards. It seemed to move with pain, arching its body and collapsing again, buzzing crossly to itself.

'Can I help?' asked the Princess.

'I do not suppose you are skilled in healing wounds such as mine. You could lift me to the edge of the Forest where I might be in the path of someone who can heal me, if she ever passes this way again. I suppose *you* are tearing blindly along the Road, like all the rest.'

'I am on a Quest, to find the single silver bird in her nest of ash-branches.'

'You could put me on a large dock-leaf, and get on your way, then. I expect you are in a hurry.'

The Princess looked about for a dock-leaf, wondering whether this irascible creature was her first test, which she was about to fail. She wiped up another tear, and plucked a particularly tough leaf, that was growing conveniently in reach of the Road.

'Good,' said the fierce little beast, rearing up and waving its legs. 'Quick now, I dislike this hole extremely. Why have you been crying?'

'Because I am not the princess who succeeds, but one of the two who fail and I don't see any way out. You won't force me to be discourteous to you, though I have remarked that your own manners are far from perfect, in that you have yet to thank me for moving the stone, and you order me here and there without saying "please", or considering that humans don't like picking up scorpions.'

She pushed the leaf towards it as she spoke, and assisted it on to it with a twig, as delicately as she could, though it wriggled and snapped furiously as she did. She put it down in the grass at the edge of the Forest.

'Most scorpions,' it observed, 'have better things to do than sting at random. If creatures like you stamp on us, then of course we retaliate. Also, if we find ourselves boxed in and afraid. But mostly we have better things to do.' It appeared to reflect for a moment. '*If* our tails are not crushed,' it added on a dejected note.

'Who is it,' the Princess enquired courteously, 'who you think can help you?'

'Oh, she is a very wise woman, who lives at the other side of the Forest. She would know what to do, but she rarely leaves home and why should she? She has everything she might want, where she is. If you were going *that* way, of couse, you could carry me a little, until I am recovered. But you are rushing headlong along the Road. Good-bye.'

The Princess was rushing nowhere; she was standing very still and thinking. She said:

'I know that story too. I carry you, and ask you, but will you not sting me? And you say, no, it is not in my interest to sting you. And when we are going along, you sting me, although we shall both suffer.

And I ask, why did you do that? And you answer –
it is my nature.'

'You are a very learned young woman, and if we
were travelling together you could no doubt tell me
many instructive stories. I might also point out that
I *cannot* sting you – my sting is disabled by the accident to my tail. You may still find me repugnant.
Your species usually does. And in any case, you are
going along this road, deviating neither to right nor
left. Good-bye.'

The Princess looked at the Scorpion. Under the
dust it was a glistening blue-black, with long arms,
fine legs and complex segments like a jet necklace.
Its claws made a crescent before its head. It was not
possible to meet its eye, which was disconcerting.

'*I* think you are very handsome.'

'Of course I am. I am quick and elegant and ver-
satile and delightfully intricate. I am surprised,
however, that you can see it.'

The Princess listened only distractedly to this
last remark. She was thinking hard. She said,
mostly to herself:

'I *could* just walk out of this inconvenient story
and go my own way. I *could* just leave the Road and

look for my own adventures in the Forest. It would make no difference to the Quest. I should have failed if I left the Road and then the next could set off. Unless of course I got turned into stone for leaving the Road.'

'I shouldn't think so,' said the Scorpion. 'And you could be very helpful to *me*, if you chose, and I know quite a few stories too, and helping other creatures is always a good idea, according to them.'

The Princess looked into the Forest. Under the green sky its green branches swayed and rustled in a beckoning way. Its mossy floor was soft and tempting after the dust and grit of the Road. The Princess bent down and lifted up the Scorpion on its leaf and put it carefully into the basket which had contained her food. Then, with a litle rebellious skip and jump, she left the Road, and set out into the trees. The Scorpion said she should go south-west, and that if she was hungry it knew where there was a thicket of brambles with early blackberries and a tree-trunk with some mushrooms, so they went in search of those, and the Princess made her mouth black without *quite* assuaging her hunger.

They travelled on, and they travelled on, in a green-arched shade, with the butterflies crowding round the Princess's head and resting on her hair and shoulders. Then they came to a shady clearing, full of grassy stumps and old dry roots, beneath one of which the Princess's keen eye detected a kind of struggling and turbulence in the sand. She stopped to see what it was, and heard a little throaty voice huskily repeating:

'Water. Oh, please, water, if you can hear me, water.'

Something encrusted with sand was crawling and flopping over the wiry roots, four helpless legs and a fat little belly. The Princess got down on her knees, ignoring the angry hissing of the Scorpion. Two liquid black eyes peered at her out of the sandy knobs, and a wide mouth opened tremulously and croaked 'Water' at her. The Princess brought out her inexhaustible water-bottle and dropped drops into the mouth and washed away the crust of sand, revealing a large and warty green and golden toad, with an unusual fleshy crest on its head. It puffed out its throat and held up its little fingers and toes to the stream of water. As the sand flowed away, it could be seen that there was a large bloody gash on the toad's head.

'Oh, you are hurt,' cried the Princess.

'I was caught,' said the Toad, 'by a Man who had been told that I carry a jewel of great value in my head. So he decided to cut it out. But that is only a story, of course, a human story told by creatures who like sticking coloured stones on their heads and skins, and all I am is flesh and blood. Fortunately for me, my skin is mildly poisonous to Men, so his fingers began to itch and puff up, and I was able to wriggle so hard that he dropped me and lost me. But I do not think that I have the strength to make my way back to the person who could heal me.'

'We are travelling in her direction,' said the Scorpion. 'You may travel with us if you care to. You could travel in this Princess's luncheon-basket, which is empty.'

'I will come gladly,' said the Toad. 'But she must not suppose I shall turn into a handsome Prince, or any such nonsense. I am a handsome Toad, or would be, if I had not been hacked at. A handsome Toad is what I shall remain.'

The Princess helped it, with a stick, to hop into her lunch-basket, and continued on through the Forest, in the direction indicated by the Scorpion. They went deeper and darker into the trees, and began to lose sense of there being paths leading anywhere. The Princess was a little tired, but the creatures kept urging her on, to go on as far as possible before night fell. In the growing gloom she almost put her foot on what looked like a ball of thread, blowing out in the roots of some thorny bushes.

The Princess stopped and bent down. *Something* was hopelessly entangled in fine black cotton, dragging itself and the knots that trapped it along in the dust. She knelt on the Forest floor and peered, and saw that it was a giant insect, with its legs and its wing-cases and its belly pulled apart by the snarled threads. The Princess, palace-bred, had never seen such a beast.

'It is a Cockroach,' observed the Scorpion. 'I thought cockroaches were too clever and tough to get into this sort of mess.'

'Those threads are a trap set by the Fowler for

singing birds,' observed the Toad. 'But he has only caught a giant Cockroach.'

The Princess disentangled some of the trailing ends, but some of the knots cut into the very substance of the creature, and she feared to damage it further. It settled stoically in the dust and let her move it. It did not speak. The Princess said:

'You had better come with us. We appear to be travelling towards someone who can heal you.'

The Cockroach gave a little shudder. The Princess picked it up, and placed it in the basket with the Scorpion and the Toad, who moved away from it fastidiously. It sat, inert, in its cocoon of black thread and said nothing.

They travelled in this way for several days, deeper into the Forest. The creatures told the Princess where to find a variety of nuts, and herbs, and berries, and wild mushrooms she would never have found for herself. Once, a long way off, they heard what seemed to be a merry human whistling, mixed with bird cries. The Princess was disposed to turn in its direction, but the Scorpion said that the whistler was the Fowler, and his calls were designed to entice unwary birds to fly into his invisible nets and to choke there. The Princess, although she was not a bird, was filled with unreasoning fear at this picture, and followed the Scorpion's instructions to creep away, deeper into the thornbushes. On another occasion, again at a distance, she heard the high, throaty sound of a horn, which reminded her of the hunting-parties in the Royal Parks, when the young courtiers would bring down deer and hares and flying fowl with their arrows, and the pretty maidens would clap their hands and exclaim. Again she thought of turning in the direction of the sound, and again, the creatures dissuaded her. For the poor Toad, when he heard the note of the horn, went sludge-grey with fear, and began to quake in the basket.

'That is the Hunter,' he said, 'who cut at my crest with his hunting-knife, who travels through the wood with cold corpses of birds and beasts strung together and cast over his shoulder, who will aim at a bright eye in a bush for pure fun, and quench it in blood. You must keep away from him.' So the Princess plunged deeper still into the thornbushes, though they were tugging at her hair and ripping her dress and scratching her pretty arms and neck.

And one day at noon the Princess heard a loud, clear voice, singing in a clearing, and, peering through a thornbush, saw a tall, brown-skinned man, naked to the waist, with black curly hair, leaning on a long axe, and singing:

> Come live with me and be my love
> And share my house and share my bed
> And you may sing from dawn to dark
> And churn the cream and bake the bread
> And lie at night in my strong arms
> Beneath a soft goosefeather spread.

The Princess was about to come out of hiding – he had such a cheery smile, and such handsome shoulders – when a dry little voice in her basket, a voice like curling wood-shavings rustling, added these lines:

> And you may scour and sweep and scrub
> With bleeding hands and arms like lead
> And I will beat your back, and drive
> My knotty fists against your head
> And sing again to other girls
> To take your place, when you are dead.

'Did you speak?' the Princess asked the Cockroach in a whisper. And it rustled back:

'I have lived in his house, which is a filthy place and full of empty beer-casks and broken bottles. He has five young wives buried in the garden, whom he attacked in his drunken rage. He doesn't kill them, he weeps drunken tears for them, but they lose their will to live. Keep away from the Wood-cutter, if you value your life.'

The Princess found this hard to believe of the Woodcutter, who seemed so lively and whole-some. She even thought that it was in the creatures' interest to prevent her from lingering with other humans, but nevertheless their warning spoke to something in her that wanted to travel onwards, so she crept quietly away again, and the Woodcutter never knew she had heard his song, or seen him standing there, looking so handsome, leaning on his axe.

They went on, and they went on, deeper into the Forest, and the Princess began to hunger most ter-ribly for bread and butter, touched perhaps by the Woodcutter's song. The berries she ate tasted more and more watery and were harder and harder to find as the Forest grew denser. The Cockroach seemed inanimate, perhaps exhausted by its effort at speech. The Princess felt bound to hurry, in case its life was in danger, and the other creatures complained from time to time of her clumsiness. Then, one evening, at the moment when the sky was taking on its deepest version of the pine-green that had succeeded dark indigo, the Scorpion begged her to stop and settle down for the night, for its tail ached intolerably. And the Toad added its croaking voice, and begged for more water to be poured over it. The Princess stopped and washed the Toad, and arranged a new leaf for the Scorpion, and said:

'Sometimes I think we shall wander like this, apparently going somewhere, in fact going nowhere, for the rest of our days.'

'In which case,' rasped the Scorpion, 'mine will not be very long, I fear.'

'I have tried to help,' said the Princess. 'But perhaps I should never have left the Road.'

And then the flaky voice was heard again.

'If you go on, and turn left, and turn left again, you will see. If you go on now.'

So the Princess took up the basket, and put her sandals back on her swollen feet, and went on, and left, and left again. And she saw, through the bushes, a dancing light, very yellow, very warm. And she went on, and saw, at a great distance, at the end of a path knotted with roots and spattered with sharp stones, a window between branches, in which a candle burned steadily. And although she had never in her cosseted life travelled far in the dark, she knew she was seeing, with a huge sense of hope, and warmth and relief, and a minor frisson of fear, what countless benighted travellers had seen before her – though against midnight-blue, not midnight-green – and she felt at one with all those lost homecomers and shelter-seekers.

'It is not the Woodcutter's cottage?' she asked the Cockroach. And it answered, sighing, 'No, no, it is the Last House, it is where we are going.'

And the Princess went on, running, and stumbling, and hopping, and scurrying, and by and by reached the little house, which was made of mossy stone, with a slate roof over low eaves and a solid wooden door above a white step. There was a good crisp smell of woodsmoke from the chimney. The

Princess was suddenly afraid – she had got used to solitude and contriving and going on – but she knocked quickly, and waited.

The door was opened by an old woman, dressed in a serviceable grey dress, with a sharp face covered with intricate fine lines like a spider's web woven of her history, which was both resolute, thoughtful, and smiling. She had sharp green eyes under hooded, purple lids, and a plaited crown of wonderful shining hair, iron-grey, silver and bright white woven together. When she opened the door the Princess almost fainted for the wonderful smell of baking bread that came out, mingled with other delicious smells, baked apples with cinnamon, strawberry tart, just-burned sugar.

'We have been waiting for you,' said the Old Woman. 'We put the candle in the window for you every night for the last week.'

She took the Princess's basket, and led her in. There was a good log fire in the chimney, with a bed of scarlet ash, and there was a long white wooden table, and there were chairs painted in dark bright colours, and everywhere there were eyes, catching the light, blinking and shining. Eyes on the mantelpiece, in the clock, behind the plates on the shelves, jet-black eyes, glass-green eyes, huge yellow eyes, amber eyes, even rose-pink eyes. And what the Princess had taken to be an intricate coloured carpet rustled and moved and shone with eyes, and revealed itself to be a mass of shifting creatures, snakes and grasshoppers, beetles and bumblebees, mice and voles and owlets and bats, a weasel and a few praying mantises. There were larger creatures too – cats and rats and badgers and kittens and a white goat. There was a low, peaceful, lively squeaking and scratching of tiny voices, welcoming and exclaiming. In one corner was a spindle and in another was a loom, and the old lady had just put aside a complicated shawl she was crocheting from a rainbow-coloured basket of scraps of wool.

'One of you needs food,' said the Old Woman, 'and three of you need healing.'

So the Princess sat down to good soup, and fresh bread, and fruit tart with clotted cream and a mug of sharp cider, and the Old Woman put the creatures on the table, and healed them in her way. Her way was to make them tell the story of their hurts, and as they told, she applied ointments and drops with tiny feathery brushes and little bone pins, uncurling and splinting the Scorpion's tail as it rasped out the tale of its injuries, swabbing and stitching the Toad's wounded head with what looked like cobweb threads, and unknotting the threads that entwined the cockroach with almost invisible hooks and tweezers. Then she asked the Princess for her story, which the Princess told as best she could, living again the moment when she realised she was doomed to fail, imitating the Scorpion's rasp, and the Toad's croaking gulp, and the husky whisper of the Cockroach. She brought the dangers of the Forest into the warm fireside, and all the creatures shuddered at the thought of the Hunter's arrow, the Fowler's snare and the Woodman's axe. And the Princess, telling the story, felt pure pleasure in getting it right, making it just so, finding the right word, and even – she went so far – the right gesture to throw shadow-branches and shadow-figures across the flickering firelight and the yellow pool of candlelight on the wall. And when she had finished there was all kinds of applause, harmonious wing-scraping, and claw-tapping, and rustling and chirruping.

'You are a born storyteller,' said the old lady. 'You had the sense to see you were caught in a story, and the sense to see that you could change it to another one. And the special wisdom to recognise that you are under a curse – which is also a blessing – which makes the story more interesting to you than the things that make it up. There are young women who would never have listened to the creatures' tales about the Woodman, but insisted on finding out for themselves. And maybe they would have been wise and maybe they would have been foolish: that is *their* story. But you listened to the Cockroach and stepped aside and came here, where we collect stories and spin stories and mend what we can and investigate what we can't, and live quietly without striving to change the world. We have no story of our own here, we are free, as old women are free, who don't have to worry about princes or kingdoms, but dance alone and take an interest in the creatures.'

'But – ' said the Princess, and stopped.

'But?'

'But the sky is still green and I have failed, and I told the story to suit myself.'

'The green is a very beautiful colour, or a very beautiful range of colours, I think,' said the old lady. 'Here, it gives us pleasure. We write songs about greenness and make tapestries with skies of every possible green. It adds to the beauty of the newt and the lizard. The Cockroach finds it restful. Why should things be as they always were?'

The Princess did not know, but felt unhappy. And the creatures crowded round to console her, and persuade her to live quietly in the little house, which was what she wanted to do, for she felt she had come home to where she was free. But she was worried about the sky and the other princesses. Then the Cockroach chirped to the old lady:

'Tell us the rest of the story, tell us the end of the story, of the story the Princess left.'

He was feeling decidedly better already, his segments were eased, and he could bend almost voluptuously.

'Well,' said the old lady, 'this is the story of the eldest Princess. But, as you percipiently observe, you can't have the story of the eldest, without the

67

stories of the next two, so I will tell you those stories, or possible stories, for many things may and do happen, stories change themselves, and these stories are not histories and have not happened. So you may believe my brief stories about the middle one and the youngest or not, as you choose.'

'I always believe stories whilst they are being told,' said the Cockroach.

'You are a wise creature,' said the Old Woman. 'That is what stories are for. And after, we shall see what we shall see.' So she told.

The brief story of the second Princess

When the second Princess realised that the first was not returning, she too set out, and met identical problems and pleasures, and sat down on the same stone, and realised that she was caught in the same story. But being a determined young woman she decided to outwit the story, and went on, and after many adventures was able to snatch the single silver bird in her nest of branches and return in triumph to her father's palace. And the old wizard told her that she must light the branches and burn the bird, and although she felt very uneasy about this she was determined to do as she should, so she lit the fire. And the nest and the bird were consumed, and a new glorious bird flew up from the conflagration, and swept the sky with its flaming tail, and everything was blue, as it had once been. And the Princess became Queen when her parents died, and ruled the people wisely, although they grumbled incessantly because they missed the variety of soft and sharp greens they had once been able to see.

The brief story of the third Princess

As for the third Princess, when the bird flamed across the sky, she went into the orchard and thought, I have no need to go on a Quest. I have nothing I must do, I can do what I like. I have no story. And she felt giddy with the empty space around her, a not entirely pleasant feeling. And a frisky little wind got up and ruffled her hair and her petticoats and blew bits of blossom all over the blue sky. And the Princess had the idea that she was tossed and blown like the petals of the cherry-trees. Then she saw an old woman, with a basket, at the gate of the orchard. So she walked towards her and when she got there, the Old Woman told her, straight out,

'You are unhappy because you have nothing to do.'

So the Princess saw that this was a wise old woman, and answered politely that this was indeed the case.

'I might help,' said the Old Woman. 'Or I might not. You may look in my basket.'

In the basket were a magic glass which would show the Princess her true love, wherever he was, whatever he was doing, and a magic loom, that made tapestries that would live on the walls of the palace chambers as though they were thickets of singing birds, and Forest rides leading to the edge of vision.

'Or I could give you a thread,' said the Old Woman, as the Princess hesitated, for she did not want to see her true love, not yet, not just yet, he was the *end* of stories not begun, and she did not want to make magic Forests, she wanted to see real ones. So she watched the old lady pick up from the grass the end of what appeared to be one of those long, trailing gossamer threads left by baby spiders travelling on the air in the early dawn. But it was as strong as linen thread, and as fine as silk, and when the Old Woman gave it a little tug it tugged tight and could be seen to run away, out of the orchard, over the meadow, into the woods and out of sight.

'You gather it in,' said the Old Woman, 'and see where it takes you.'

The thread glittered and twisted, and the Princess began to roll it neatly in, and took a few steps along it, and gathered it, and rolled it into a ball, and followed it, out of the orchard, across the meadow, and into the woods, and ... but that is another story.

'Tell me one thing,' said the eldest Princess to the Old Woman, when they had all applauded her story. The moon shone in an emerald sky, and all the creatures drowsed and rustled. 'Tell me one thing. Was that you, ahead of me in the road, in such a hurry?'

'There is always an old woman ahead of you on a journey, and there is always an old woman behind you too, and they are not always the same, and may be fearful or kindly, dangerous or delightful, as the road shifts, and you speed along it. Certainly I was ahead of you, and behind you too, but not only I, and not only as I am now.'

'I am happy to be here with you as you are now.'

'Then that is a good place to go to sleep, and stop telling stories until the morning, which will bring its own changes.'

So they went to bed, and slept until the sun streaked the apple-green horizon with grassy-golden light.

Dragons' Breath

Dragon, from *Die Bilder zur Bibel*,
Matthäus Merian, 1593-1650

Dragons' Breath

Once upon a time, in a village in a valley surrounded by high mountains, lived a family with two sons and a daughter, whose names were Harry, Jack and Eva. The village was on the lower slopes of the mountains, and in the deep bowl of the valley was a lake, clear as crystal on its shores, and black as ink in its unplumbed centre. Thick pine forests grew in the shadow of the mountain ridges, but the village stood amongst flowery meadows and orchards, and cornfields, not luscious, but sufficient for the needs of the villagers. The peaks of the mountains were inaccessible, with blue ice-shadows and glittering snow-fields. The sides of the mountain were scored with long descending channels, like the furrows of some monstrous plough. In England the circular impressions around certain hills are ascribed to the coiling grip of ancient dragons, and in that country there was a tale that in some primeval time the channels had been cut by the descent of giant worms from the peaks. In the night, by the fire, parents frightened children pleasurably with tales of the flaming, cavorting descent of the dragons.

Harry, Jack and Eva were not afraid of dragons, but they were, in their different ways, afraid of boredom. Life in that village repeated itself, generation after generation. They were born, they became lovers, they became parents and grandparents, they died. They were somewhat inbred, to tell the truth, for the outside world was far away, and hard to reach, and only a few traders came and went, in the summer months, irregularly. The villagers made a certain traditional kind of rug, on handlooms, with a certain limited range of colours from vegetable dyes they made themselves – a blood-red, a dark blue with a hint of green, a sandy yellow, a charcoal black. There were a few traditional designs, which hardly varied: a branching tree, with fruit like pomegranates, and roosting birds, somewhat like pheasants, or a more abstract geometrical design, with discs of one colour threaded on a crisscrossing web of another on the ground of a third. The rugs were on the whole made by the women, who also cooked and washed. The men looked after the livestock, worked the fields and made music. They had their own musical instrument, a wailing pipe, not found anywhere else, though most of them had not travelled far enough to know that.

Harry was a swineherd and Jack dug in the fields, sowed and harvested. Harry had a particular friend amongst the pigs, a young boar called Boris, a sagacious creature who made cunning escapes and dug up unexpected truffles. But Boris's playfulness was not enough to mitigate Harry's prevailing boredom. He dreamed of great cities beyond the mountain, with streaming crowds of urgent people, all different, all busy. Jack liked to see the corn come up, green spikes in the black earth, and he knew where to find ceps and wild honey, but these treats did little to mitigate his prevailing boredom. He dreamed of ornamental gardens inside high walls surrounding huge palaces. He dreamed of subtle tastes, spices and fiery spirits unknown in the valley. He dreamed also of wilder dances, bodies flung about freely, to music on instruments he knew only by hearsay: the zither, the bongo drum, the grand piano, tubular bells.

Eva made the rugs. She could have woven in her sleep, she thought, and often did, waking to find her mind buzzing with repeats and variations, twisting threads and shifting warp and weft. She dreamed of unknown colours, purple, vermilion, turquoise and orange, colours of flowers and feathers, soft silks, sturdy cottons. She dreamed of an older Eva, robed in crimson and silver. She dreamed of the sea, which she could not imagine, she dreamed of salt water and tasted her own impatient tears. She was not good at weaving, she made her tension too tight, and her patterns bunched, but this was her task. She was a weaver. She wanted to be a traveller, a sailor, a learned doctor, an opera singer in front of flaring footlights and the roar of the crowd.

The first sign may have been the hunters' reports of unusual snow-slides in the high mountains. Or maybe it was, as some of them later claimed, dawns that were hectically rosy, sunsets that flared too crimson. They began to hear strange rumblings and crackings up there, above the snow-line, which they discussed, as they discussed every strange and every accustomed sound, with their repetitious measuring commentary that made Jack and Harry grind their teeth with rage at the sameness of it all. After a time it became quite clear that the rim of the mountains directly above the village, both by day and by night, was flickering and dancing with a kind of fiery haze, a smoky salmon-pink, a burst here and there of crimson and gold. The colours were rather beautiful, they agreed as they watched from their doorsteps, the bright ribbons of colour flashing through the grey-blue smokiness of the air, and then subsiding. Below this flaming rim the white of the snow was giving way to the gaunt grey of wet rock, and the shimmer – and yes, steam – of new water.

They must have been afraid from the beginning: they could see well enough that large changes were taking place, that everything was on the move, earth and air, fire and water. But the fear was mixed with a great deal of excited *interest*, and with even a certain pleasure in novelty, and with aesthetic pleasure, of which many of them were later ashamed. Hunting-parties went out in the direction of the phenomenon and came back to report that the hill-side seemed to be on the move, and was boiling and burning, so that it was hard to see through the very thick clouds of ash and smoke and steam that hung over the movement. The mountains were not, as far as anyone knew, volcanic, but the lives of men are short beside the history of rocks and stones, so they wondered and debated.

After some time they saw on the skyline lumps like the knuckles of a giant fist, six lumps, where nothing had been, lumps that might represent objects the size of large sheds or small houses, at that distance. And over the next few weeks the lumps advanced, in smoke and spitting sparks, regularly and slowly, side by side, without hesitation or deviation, down the mountainside. Behind each tump trailed a long, unbending tube, as it were, or furrow-ridge, or earth-work, coming over the crest of the mountain, over the rim of their world, pouring slowly on and down.

Some brave men went out to prospect but were forced back by clouds of scalding steam and showers of burning grit. Two friends, bold hunters both, went out and never returned.

One day a woman in her garden said: – 'It is almost as though it was not landslides but creatures, great worms with fat heads creeping down on us. Great fat, nodding bald heads, with knobs and spouts and whelks and whorls on them, and nasty hot wet eyes in great caverns in their muddy flesh, that glint blood-red, twelve eyes, can you see them, and twelve hairy nostrils on blunt snouts made of grey mud.' And after conversations and comparisons and pointings and descriptions they could all see them, and they were just as she said, six fat, lolling, loathsome heads, trailing heavy bodies as long as the road from their village to the next, trailing them with difficulty, even with pain, it seemed, but unrelenting and deadly slow.

When they were nearer – and the slowness of their progress was dreamlike, unreal – their great jaws could be seen, jaws wide as whales and armed with a scythe-like horny or flinty edge like a terrible beak, with which they excavated and swallowed a layer of the earth and whatever was on it – bushes, fences, haystacks, fruit trees, a couple of goats, a black and white cow, a duckpond and the life in it. They sucked and scythed, with a soughing noise, and they spat out fine ash, or dribbled it from the lips of the terrible jaws, and it settled on everything. As they approached, the cloud of ash came before them, and settled on everything in the houses and gardens, coated the windows, filmed the wells. It stank, the ash, it was unspeakably foul. At first they grumbled and dusted, and then they gave up dusting, for it was no use, and began to be afraid. It was all so slow that there was a period of unreal, half-titillating fear, before the real, sick, paralysing fear took hold, which was when the creatures were close enough for men and women to see their eyes, which were rimmed with a gummy discharge, like melting rubber, and their tongues of flame. The tongues of flame were nothing like the brave red banners of painted dragons in churches, and nothing like the flaming swords of archangels. They were molten and lolling, covered with a leathery transparent skin thick with crimson warts and taste-buds glowing like coals, the size of cabbages, slavering with some sulphurous glue and stinking of despair and endless decay that would never be clean again in

the whole life of the world. Their bodies were re-
pulsive, as they humped and slithered and crushed,
slow and grey and indiscriminate. Their faces were
too big to be seen as faces – only identified in parts,
successively. But the stench was the worst thing,
and the stench induced fear, then panic, then a
fatalistic tremor of paralysis, like rabbits before
stoats, or mice before vipers.

The villagers discussed for far too long the
chances of the village being destroyed. They discussed also expedients for diverting, or damaging
the worms, but these were futile, and came to
nothing. They discussed also the line of the
creatures' advance; whether it crossed the village,
or whether it might be projected to pass by it on
one side or another. Afterwards it might have been
easy to agree that it was always clear that the village stood squarely in the path of that terrible
descent, but hope misleads, and inertia misleads,
and it is hard to imagine the vanishing of what has
seemed as stable as stone. So the villagers left it
very late to make a plan to evacuate their village,
and in the end left hurriedly and messily, running
here and there in the stink and smoke of that bad

breath, snatching up their belongings, putting them down and snatching up others, seething like an ants' nest. They ran into the forest with sacks of corn and cooking-pots, with feather-beds and sides of bacon, completely bewildered by the presence of the loathsome creatures. It was not clear that the worms exactly saw the human beings. The human beings were not on their scale, as small creatures that inhabit our scalps, or burrow in the salad leaves we eat are not visible to us, and we take no account of them.

The villagers' life in the forest became mono-tonous, boring even, since boredom is possible for human beings in patches of tedium between exer-tion and terror. They were very cold, especially at night, they were hungry and their stomachs were constantly queasy, both with fear and with their ramshackle diet. They knew they were beyond the perimeter of the worms' breath, and yet they smelt its foul odour, in their dreams, in the curl of smoke from their camp-fires, in rotting leaves. They had watchers posted, who were placed to be able to see in the distance the outline of the village, who saw the line of gross heads advancing imperceptibly, who saw bursts of sudden flame and spurts of dense smoke that must have been the kindling of houses. They were watching the destruction of their world, and yet they felt a kind of ennui which was part of all the other distress they felt. You might ask – where were the knights, where were the warriors who would at least ride out and try to put an arrow or a bullet through those drooling eyes. There was talk of this round the camp-fires, but no heroes sprang up, and it is probable that this was wise, that the things were invulnerable to the pinprick of human weapons. The elders said it was best to let things go by, for those huge bodies would be almost as noisome dead as alive in the village midst. The old women said that old tales told that dragons' breath paralysed the will, but when they were asked for practical advice, *now*, they had none to offer. You could want to kill yourself, Eva found out, because you were sleeping on a tree-root, on the hard ground, which pressed into your flesh and became an excruciating pain, boring in both senses.

Harry and Jack finally went with some other young

men, out in the direction of the village, to see from
close quarters the nature and extent of the devastation. They found they were walking towards a
whole wall of evil-smelling smoke and flame, extending across acres of pastureland and cornfield,
behind which the great crag-like protuberances of
the heads could be seen, further apart now, moving
on like the heads of water at the mouth of a flood-
ing delta. Jack said to Harry that this fanning-out of
the paths left little chance that anything in the village might be left standing, and Harry replied
distractedly that there were figures of some sort
moving in the smoke, and then said that they were
the pigs, running here and there, squealing. A pig
shot out of the smoke, panting and squeaking, and
Harry called out, 'Boris!' and began to run after his
pig, which snorted wildly and charged back into
the darkness, followed by Harry, and Jack saw pig
and human in sooty silhouette before he heard a
monstrous sucking sound, and an exhalation of hot
vapours and thick, choking fiery breath which sent
him staggering and fainting back. When he came
to, his skin was thick with adhesive ash and he

could hear, it seemed to him, the liquids boiling and burning in the worm's belly.

For a moment he thought he would simply lie there, in the path of that jaw, and be scooped up with the cornfield and the hedgerow. Then he found he had decided to roll away, and little by little, rolling, crawling and scrambling, he put patches of space between himself and the worm. He lay for several hours, then, winded and sick, under a thornbush, before picking himself painfully up, and returning to the camp in the forest. He hoped that Harry too would return, but was not surprised, not really surprised, when he did not.

And so it dragged on, for weeks and months, with the air full of ash and falling cinders, with their clothes and flesh permeated by that terrible smell, until little by little the long loathsome bodies dragged past, across the fields and the meadows, leaving behind those same furrows of rocky surface, scooped clean of life and growth. And from a hilly point they saw the creatures, side by side, cross the sandy shore of the lake, and without changing pace or hesitating, advance across the shallows, as though driven by mechanical necessity, or by some organic need like the periodic return of toads or turtles to a watery world to breed. And the great heads dipped to meet the lake surface, and where they met it, it boiled, and steamed and spat like a great cauldron. And then the heads went under the surface, which still boiled, puckered and bubbling, as the slow lengths of the long bodies humped and slithered, day after day over the sand and down through the water to the depths, until finally only blunt, ugly butts could be seen, under the shallows, and then one day, as uncertainly as their coming had been established, it became clear that their going was over, that the worms had plunged into, through, under the lake, leaving only the harsh marks of their bodies' weight and burning breath in the soil, the rock, the vegetable world crushed and withered.

When the villagers returned to look on their village from a distance, the devastation seemed uniform: the houses flattened, the trees uprooted, the earth scored, channelled, ashy and smoking. They wandered in the ruins, turning over bricks and boards, some people finding, as some people always will, lost treasures and trivia in the ashes, a coin, half a book, a dented cooking-pot. And some people who had vanished in the early chaos returned, with singed eyebrows or seared faces, and others did not. Jack and Eva came back together, and for a moment could not work out in what direction to look for the ruins of what had been their house. And then, coming round a heap of fallen rubble they saw it there, untouched. One of the dragon-troughs passed at a distance, parallel to the garden fence, but the fence stood, and inside the fence the garden, the veranda, the doors and windows were as they had always been, apart from the drifting ash. And Jack lifted the stone under which the key was always kept, and there was the key, where it had always been. And Jack and Eva went into the house, and there were tables and chairs, fireplace and bookcase, and Eva's loom, standing in the window, at the back of the house, where you looked out on the slopes and then up at the peaks of the mountains. And there was a heavy humping sound against the back door, which Jack opened. And when he opened it, there was Boris the pig, hanging his head a little, and giving off an odour of roast pork, with not a bristle on his charred rind, but with pleasure and recognition in his deepset little eyes.

When they saw that the pig had by some miracle, or kindness of luck, escaped the dragon-breath and the fiery tongues, they hoped, of course, that Harry too would return. They hoped he would return for days and months, and against their reasonable judgment, for years. But he did not.

Eva dusted her rug, which was lightly filmed with ash, since it was at the back of the house, and the windows were well-made. She saw the colours – red, blue, yellow, black – as though she had never seen colour before, and yet with disturbed pleasure at their familiarity. An archaeologist, finding this room, and this rug on this loom in it, say two thousand years later, might have felt intense excitement that these things were improbably intact, and intense curiosity about the workmanship, and about the even daily life that could be partly imagined around the found artefacts. Eva felt such amazement now, about her own work, the stubborn persistence of wood and wool and bone shuttle, or the unfinished tree with its squatting pheasants and fat pomegranates. She felt inwardly moved and shaken, also, by this form of her own past, and the past of her mother and grandmother, and by the traces of her moments of flowing competence, and of her periods of bunching, tension, anxiety, fumbling. Jack too felt delight and amazement, walking repeatedly across the house from the windows which opened on smouldering devastation to those from which you could see the unchanging mountains. Both embraced Boris, restored and rescued, feeling his wet snout and warm flanks. Such wonder, such amazement, are the opposite, the exact opposite, of boredom, and many people only know them after fear and loss. Once known, I believe, they cannot be completely forgotten; they cast flashes and floods of paradisal light in odd places and at odd times.

The villagers rebuilt their village, and the rescued things in the rescued house stood amongst new houses in whose gardens new flowers and vegetables sprouted, and new saplings were planted.

The people began to tell tales about the coming of the worms down the mountain, and the tales too were the opposite of boredom. They made ash and bad breath, crushing and swallowing, interesting, exciting, almost beautiful. Some things they made into tales, and some things they did not speak. Jack told of Harry's impetuous bravery, rushing into the billowing smoke to save his pig, and nobody told the day-to-day misery of the slowly diminishing hope of his return. The resourcefulness and restoration of the pig were celebrated, but not his inevitable fate, in these hard days. And these tales, made from those people's wonder at their own survival, became in time, charms against boredom for their children and grandchildren, riddling hints of the true relations between peace and beauty and terror.

The Djinn in the Nightingale's Eye

Turkish djinn shadow puppet

The Djinn in the Nightingale's Eye

Once upon a time, when men and women hurtled through the air on metal wings, when they wore webbed feet and walked on the bottom of the sea, learning the speech of whales and the songs of the dolphins, when pearly-fleshed and jewelled apparitions of Texan herdsmen and houris shimmered in the dusk on Nicaraguan hillsides, when folk in Norway and Tasmania in dead of winter could dream of fresh strawberries, dates, guavas and passion fruits and find them spread next morning on their tables, there was a woman who was largely irrelevant, and therefore happy.

Her business was storytelling, but she was no ingenious queen in fear of the shroud brought in with the dawn, nor was she a naquibolmalek to usher a shah through the gates of sleep, nor an ashik, lover-minstrel singing songs of Mehmet the Conqueror and the sack of Byzantium, nor yet a holy dervish in short skin trousers and skin skull-cap, brandishing axe or club and making its shadow terrible. She was no meddah, telling incredible tales in the Ottoman court or the coffee-houses by the market. She was merely a narratologist, a being of secondary order, whose days were spent hunched in great libraries scrying, interpreting, decoding the fairy-tales of childhood and the vodka-posters of the grown-up world, the unending romances of golden coffee-drinkers, and the impeded couplings of doctors and nurses, dukes and poor maidens, horsewomen and musicians. Sometimes also, she flew. In her impoverished youth she had supposed that scholarship was dry, dusty and static, but now she knew better. Two or three times a year she flew to strange cities, to China, Mexico and Japan, to Transylvania, Bogota and the South Seas, where narratologists gathered like starlings, parliaments of wise fowls, telling stories about stories.

At the time when my story begins the green sea was black, sleek as the skins of killer whales, and the sluggish waves were on fire, with dancing flames and a great curtain of stinking smoke. The empty deserts were seeded with skulls, and with iron canisters, containing death. Pestilence crept invisibly from dune to dune. In those days men and women, including narratologists, were afraid to fly East, and their gatherings were diminished. Nevertheless our narratologist, whose name was Gillian Perholt, found herself in the air, between London and Ankara. Who can tell if she travelled because she was English and stolid and could not quite imagine being blasted out of the sky, or because, although she was indeed an imaginative being, and felt an appropriate measure of fear, she could not resist the idea of the journey above the clouds, above the minarets of Istanbul, and the lure of seeing the Golden Horn, the Bosphorus and the shores of Europe and Asia face to face? Flying is statistically safer than any other travel, Gillian Perholt told herself, and surely at this time, only slightly less safe, statistically only a little less.

She had a phrase for the subtle pleasures of solitary air travel. She spoke it to herself like a charm as the great silver craft detached itself from its umbilical tube at Heathrow, waddled like an albatross across the tarmac and went up, up, through grey curtains of English rain, a carpet of woolly iron-grey

English cloud, a world of swirling vapour, trailing its long limbs and scarves past her tiny porthole, in the blue and gold world that was always there, above the grey, always. 'Floating redundant' she said to herself, sipping champagne, nibbling salted almonds, whilst all round her spread the fields of heaven, white and rippling, glistening and gleaming, rosy and blue in the shadows, touched by the sun with steady brightness. 'Floating redundant', she murmured blissfully as the vessel banked and turned and a disembodied male voice spoke in the cabin, announcing that there was a veil of water vapour over France but that that would burn off, and then they would see the Alps, when the time came. Burn off was a powerful term, she thought, rhetorically interesting, for water does not burn and yet the sun's heat reduces this water to nothing; I am in the midst of fierce forces. I am nearer the sun than any woman of my kind, any ancestress of mine, can ever have dreamed of being, I can look in his direction and stay steadily here, floating redundant.

The phrase was, of course, not her own; she was, as I have said, a being of a secondary order. The phrase was John Milton's, plucked from the air, or the circumambient language, at the height of his powers, to describe the beauty of the primordial coils of the insinuating serpent in the Paradise garden. Gillian Perholt remembered the very day these words had first coiled into shape and risen in beauty from the page, and struck at her, unsuspecting as Eve. There she was, sixteen years old, a golden-haired white virgin with vague blue eyes (she pictured herself so) and there on the ink-stained desk in the dust was the battered emerald-green book, inkstained too, and second-hand, scribbled across and across by dutiful or impatient female fingers, and everywhere was a smell, still drily pungent, of hot ink and linoleum and dust if not ashes, and there he was, the creature, insolent and lovely before her.

> not with indented wave,
> Prone on the ground, as since, but on his rear,
> Circular base of rising folds, that towered
> Fold above fold a surging maze, his head
> Crested aloft and carbuncle his eyes;
> With burnished neck of verdant gold, erect
> Amidst his circling spires, that on the grass

Floated redundant: pleasing was his shape,
And lovely.

And for an instant Gillian Perholt had *seen*, brilliant
and swaying, not the snake Eve had seen in the garden, nor yet the snake that had risen in the dark
cave inside the skull of blind John Milton, but a
snake, the snake, the same snake, in some sense,
made of words and visible to the eye. So, as a child,
from time to time, she had *seen* wolves, bears and
small grey men, standing between her and the
safety of the door, or her father's sleeping Sunday
form in an armchair. But I digress, or am about to
digress. I called up the snake (I saw him too, in my
time) to explain Dr Perholt's summing-up of her
own state.

In those days she had been taught to explain
'floating redundant' as one of Milton's magical fus-
ings of two languages – 'floating', which was
Teutonic and to do with floods, and 'redundant',
which was involved and Latinate, and to do with
overflowings. Now she brought to it her own wit, a
knowledge of the modern sense of 'redundant',
which was to say, superfluous, unwanted, un-
necessary, let go. 'I'm afraid we shall have to let

you go,' employers said, everywhere, offering freedom to reluctant Ariels, as though the employees were captive sprites, only too anxious to rush uncontrolled into the elements. Dr Perholt's wit was only secondarily to do with employment, however. It was primarily to do with her sex and age, for she was a woman in her fifties, past child-bearing, whose two children were adults now, had left home and had left England, one for Saskatchewan and one for São Paulo, from where they communicated little, for they were occupied with children of their own. Dr Perholt's husband also, had left home, had left Dr Perholt, had removed himself after two years of soul-searching, two years of scurrying in and out of his/their home, self-accusation, irritability, involuntary impotence, rejection of lovingly cooked food, ostentatious display of concealed messages, breathed phone-calls when Dr Perholt appeared to be sleeping, missed dinner engagements, mysterious dips in the balance at the bank, bouts of evil-smelling breath full of brandy and stale smoke, also of odd-smelling skin, with touches of alien sweat, hyacinths and stephanotis. He had gone to Majorca with Emmeline Porter and from there had sent a fax message to Gillian Perholt, saying he was a coward for doing it this way, but it was also done to save her, and that he was never coming home.

Gillian Perholt happened to be in her study when the fax began to manifest itself, announced by a twangling bell and a whirring sound. It rose limp and white in the air and flopped exhausted over the edge of the desk – it was long and self-exculpatory, but there is no need for me to recount it to you, you can imagine it very well for yourself. Equally, you can imagine Emmeline Porter for yourself, she has no more to do with this story. She was twenty-six, that is all you need to know, and more or less what you supposed, probably, anyway. Gillian watched the jerky progress and flopping of the fax with admiration, not for Mr Perholt's fluency, but for the way in which agitated black scribbling could be fed into a machine slit in Majorca and appear simultaneously in Primrose Hill. The fax had been bought for Mr Perholt, an editorial consultant, to work from home when he was let go or made redundant in the banal sense, but its main user was Gillian

Perholt, who received E-mail and story variants from narratologists in Cairo and Auckland, Osaka and Port of Spain. Now the fax was hers, since he was gone. And although she was now redundant as a woman, being neither wife, mother nor mistress, she was by no means redundant as a narratologist but on the contrary, in demand everywhere. For this was a time when women were privileged, when female narratologists had skills greatly revered, when there were pythonesses, abbesses and sibyls in the world of narratology, who revealed mysteries and kept watch at the boundaries of correctness.

On receiving the fax, Gillian Perholt stood in the empty study and imagined herself grieving over betrayal, the loss of love, the loss of companionship perhaps, of respect in the world, maybe, as an ageing woman rejected for one more youthful. It was a sunny day in Primrose Hill, and the walls of the study were a cheerful golden colour, and she saw the room fill up with golden light and felt full of lightness, happiness and purpose. She felt, she poetically put it to herself, like a prisoner bursting chains and coming blinking out of a dungeon. She felt like a bird confined in a box, like a gas confined in a bottle, that found an opening, and rushed out. She felt herself expand in the space of her own life. No more waiting for meals. No more grumbling and jousting, no more exhausted anticipation of alien feelings, no more snoring, no more farts, no more trace of stubble in the washbasin.

She considered her reply. She wrote:

OK. Agreed. Clothes in bales in store. Books in chests ditto. Will change locks. Have a good time. G.

She knew she was lucky. Her ancestresses, about whom she thought increasingly often, would probably have been dead by the age she had reached. Dead in childbed, dead of influenza, or tuberculosis, or puerperal fever, or simple exhaustion, dead, as she travelled back in time, from worn-out unavailing teeth, from cracked kneecaps, from hunger, from lions, tigers, sabre-toothed tigers, invading aliens, floods, fires, religious persecution, human sacrifice, why not? Certain female narratologists talked with pleasurable awe about wise Crones but she was no crone, she was an unprecedented being, a woman with porcelain-crowned teeth, laser-corrected vision, her own store of money, her own life and field of power, who flew, who slept in luxurious sheets around the world, who gazed out at the white fields under the sun by day and the brightly turning stars by night as she floated redundant.

The conference in Ankara was called 'Stories of Women's Lives'. This was a pantechnicon title to make space for everyone, from every country, from every genre, from every time. Dr Perholt was met at the airport by an imposing bearded Turkish professor, dark and smiling, into whose arms she rushed with decorous cries of joy, for he was an old friend, they had been students together amongst mediaeval towers and slow, willow-bordered rivers, they had a story of their own, a very minor sub-plot, a thread now tenuous, now stronger, but never broken, in the tapestry of both lives. Dr Perholt was angry at the blonde Lufthansa hostess who bowed gravely to the grey businessmen as they disembarked, goodbye, sir and thank you, good-bye, sir and thank you, but gave Dr Perholt a condescending 'Bye-bye, dear.' But Orhan Rifat, beyond the airport threshold, was as always alive with projects, new ideas, new poems, new discoveries. They would visit Izmir with a group of Turkish friends. Gillian would then visit Istanbul, his city.

The conference, like most conferences, resembled a bazaar, where stories and ideas were exchanged and changed. It took place in a cavernous theatre with no windows on the outside world but well provided with screens where transparencies flickered fitfully in the dark. The best narratologists work by telling and retelling tales. This holds the hearer from sleep and allows the teller to insert him- or herself into the tale. Thus a fierce Swiss writer told the horrid story of Typhoid Mary, an innocent polluter, an unwitting killer. Thus the elegant Leyla Doruk added passion and flamboyance to her version of the story of the meek Fanny Price, trembling and sickly in the deepest English wooded countryside. Orhan Rifat was to speak last: his title was 'Powers and powerlessness: djinns and women in *The Arabian Nights.*' Gillian Perholt spoke before him. She had chosen to analyse the Clerk's Tale from *The Canterbury Tales*, which is the story of Patient Griselda. No one has ever much liked this story, although it is told by one of Chaucer's most sympathetic pilgrims, the book-loving, unworldly Clerk of Oxford, who took it from Petrarch's Latin, which was a rendering of Boccaccio's Italian. Gillian Perholt did not like this story; that was why she had chosen to tell it, amongst the stories of women's lives. What do I think of, she had asked herself, on receiving the invitation, when I think of 'Stories of Women's Lives', and had answered herself with a thrill and a shudder, 'Patient Griselda'.

So now she told it, in Ankara, to a mixed audience of scholars and students. Most of the Turkish students were like students everywhere, in jeans and tee-shirts, but conspicuous in the front row were three young women with their heads wrapped in grey scarves, and dotted amongst the young men in jeans were soldiers – young officers – in uniform. In the secular Turkish republic the scarves were a sign of religious defiance, an act of independence with which liberal-minded Turkish professors felt they should feel sympathy, though in a Muslim state much of what they themselves taught and cared about would be as objectionable, as forbidden, as the covered heads were here. The young soldiers, Gillian Perholt observed, listened intently and took assiduous notes. The three scarved women, on the other hand, stared proudly ahead, never meeting the speakers' eyes, as though completely preoccupied with their own conspicuous self-assertion. They came to hear all the speakers. Orhan had asked one of them, he told Gillian, why she dressed as she did. 'My father and my fiancé say it is right,' she had said. 'And I agree.'

The story of Patient Griselda, as told by Gillian Perholt, is this.

There was once a young marquis, in Lombardy, whose name was Walter. He enjoyed his life, and his sports – hunting and hawking – as young men do, and had no desire to marry, perhaps because marriage appeared to him to be a form of confinement, or possibly because marriage is the end of youth, and its freedom from care, if youth is free from care. However his people came and urged him to take a wife, perhaps, as they told him, because he should think of begetting an heir, perhaps because they felt marriage would steady him. He professed himself moved by their arguments and invited them to his wedding, on a certain day he fixed on – with the condition that they swore to accept this bride, whoever she might be.

It was one of Walter's peculiarities that he liked to make people swear in advance to accept unconditionally and without repining whatever he himself might choose to do.

So the people agreed and made ready for the wedding on the chosen day. They made a feast and prepared rich clothes, jewels and bedlinen for the unknown bride. And on the chosen day the priest was waiting, and the bridal procession mounted, and still no one knew who the bride was to be.

Now Griseldis, or Grisilde, or Grisildis or Grissel or Griselda was the daughter of a poor peasant. She was both beautiful and virtuous. On the day fixed for the wedding she set out to fetch water from the well; she had all the domestic virtues and meant to finish her housework before standing in the lane with the other peasants to cheer as the bridal procession wound past. Weddings make spectators – participating spectators – of us all. Griselda wanted to be part of the wedding, and to look at the bride, as we all do. We all like to look at brides. Brides and princesses, those inside the story, imagined from the outside. Who knows but Griselda was looking forward to imagining the feelings of this unknown woman as she rode past.

Only the young Lord rode up, and did not ride past, but stopped, and made her put down her pitcher, and wait. And he spoke to her father, and said that it was his intention to make Griselda his wife, if her father would give his consent to her will. So the young Lord spoke to the young woman and said he wanted to make her his bride, and that his only requirement was that she should promise to obey him in everything, to do whatever he desired, without hesitating or repining, at every moment of the day or night. And Griselda, 'qua-kynge for drede' as Chaucer tells us, swore that never willingly, in act or thought, would she disobey him, on pain of death – though she would fear to die, she told the young Lord.

And then young Walter commanded immediately that her clothes should be taken off and that she should be clothed in the rich new garments he had prepared, with her hair dressed and her head crowned with a jewelled coronet. And so she went away to be married, and to live in the castle, and Chaucer tells us, he takes care to tell us, that she showed great qualities of judgment, reconciliation of disputes, bounty and courtesy in her new position, and was much loved by the people.

But the story goes inexorably on, past the wedding, into the ominous future foreshadowed by the pledge exacted and vouchsafed. And consider this, said Gillian Perholt at this point in the story:- in almost all stories of promises and prohibitions, the promises and prohibitions carry with them the inevitability of failure, of their own breaking. Orhan Rifat smiled into his beard, and the soldiers wrote rapidly, presumably about promises and prohibitions, and the grey-scarved women stared fixedly ahead.

After a time, Chaucer says, Griselda gave birth to a daughter, although she would rather have borne a son; but everyone rejoiced, for once it is seen that a woman is not barren, a son may well come next. And at this point it came into Walter's head that he must test his wife. It is interesting, said Gillian, that here the Clerk of Oxford dissociates himself as narrator from his protagonist, and says he cannot see why this testing seemed to be necessary. But he goes on to tell how Walter informed his wife gravely that the people grumbled at having a peasant's daughter set over them, and did not want such a person's child to be set above them. He therefore proposed, he said, to put her daughter to death. And Griselda answered that she and her child were his to do with as he thought best. So Walter sent a rough sergeant to take the child, from the breast. And Griselda kissed it goodbye, asking only that the baby should be buried where wild creatures could not tear it.

And after a further time, Griselda gave birth to a son, and the husband, still intent on testing, had this child too taken from the breast and carried away to be killed. And Griselda kept steadily to her pact, assuring him that she was not grieved or hurt;

that her two children had brought her only sickness at first 'and after, woe and pain'.

And then there was a lull in the narrative, said Gillian, a lull long enough for the young children who were secretly being brought up in Bologna to reach puberty, adolescence, a marriageable age. A lull as long as the space between Acts III and IV of *A Winter's Tale* during which Hermione the Queen is hidden away and thought to be dead, and her daughter, Perdita, abandoned and exposed, is brought up by shepherds, wooed by a Prince, and forced to flee to Sicily where she is happily reunited with her repentant father and her lost mother who appears on a pedestal as a statue and is miraculously given her life and happiness again by art. In the *Winter's Tale*, said Gillian, the lovely daughter is the renewal of the mother, as the restoration of Persephone was the renewal of the fields in Spring, laid waste by the rage of Demeter, the mother-goddess. Here Gillian's voice faltered. She looked out at the audience and told them how Paulina, Hermione's friend and servant, had taken on the powers of witch, artist, storyteller, and had restored the lost queen to life. Personally, said

Gillian, I have never been able to stomach – to bear – that plotted dénouement, which is the opposite of the restoration of Persephone in Spring. For human beings do not die and spring up again like the grass and the corn, they live one life and get older. And from Hermione – and as you may know already, from Patient Griselda – most of that life has been taken by plotting, has been made into a grey void of forced inactivity.

What did Griselda do whilst her son, and more particularly her daughter were growing up? The story gallops. A woman's life runs from wedding to childbirth to nothing in a twinkling of an eye. Chaucer gives no hint of subsequent children, though he insists that Griselda remained true in love and patience and submission. But her husband had to excess Paulina's desire to narrate, to orchestrate, to direct. He busied himself, he gained a dispensation from the Pope to put away his wife Griselda, and to marry a young bride. The people muttered about the murdered children. But Walter, if we are to believe the story, went to his patient wife and told her that he intended to replace her with a younger and more acceptable bride, and that she must return to her father, leaving behind the rich clothes and jewels and other things which had been his gift. And still Griselda was patient, though Chaucer here gives her words of power in her patience which keep the reader's sympathy, and fend off the reader's impatience which might sever that sympathy.

Naked, Griselda tells her husband, she came from her father, and naked she will return. But since he has taken all her old clothes she asks him for a smock to cover her nakedness, since 'the womb in which your children lay, should not, as I walk, be seen bare before the people. Let me not,' says Griselda, 'go by the way like a worm. In exchange for my maidenhead which I brought with me and cannot take away, give me a smock.' And Walter graciously allows her the shift she stands in, to cover her nakedness.

But Walter thought of other twists to the intrigue, since every twist made his plotted dénouement more splendid and satisfactory. No sooner, it seemed, was Griselda back at home, than her husband was there, asking her to return to the castle and prepare the rooms and the feast for his new young bride. No one could do it better, he told her. You might think that the pact was over on her return to her father's house, but this was not Griselda's idea: patiently she returned, patiently she cooked, cleaned, prepared, made up the marriage bed.

And the bridal procession arrived at the castle, with the beautiful girl in the midst, and Griselda worked away in the hall in her poor clothes, and the feast was set, and the lords and ladies sat down to eat. Now indeed, apparently, Griselda was a belated spectator at the wedding. Walter called Griselda to him and asked her what she thought of his wife and her beauty. And Griselda did not curse her, or indeed him, but answered always patiently, that she had never seen a fairer woman, and that she both beseeched and warned him 'never to prick this tender maiden with tormenting' as he had done her, for the young bride was softly brought up and would not endure it.

And now Walter had his dénouement, the end of his story, and revealed to Griselda that his bride was not his bride, but her daughter, and the squire her son, and that all would now be well and she would be happy, for he had done all this neither in malice nor in cruelty, but to test her good faith, which he had not found wanting. So now they could be reconciled.

And what did Griselda do? asked Gillian Perholt? And what did she say, and what did she do? repeated Dr Perholt. Her audience was interested. It was not a story most of them knew beyond the title and its idea, Patient Griselda. Would the worm turn? one or two asked themselves, moved by Griselda's image of her own naked flesh. They looked up to Dr Perholt for an answer, and she was silent, as if frozen. She stood on the stage, her mouth open to speak, and her hand out, in a rhetorical gesture, with the lights glittering on her eyeballs. She was am ample woman, a stout woman, with a soft clear skin, clothed in the kind of draped linen dress and jacket that is best for stout women, a stone-coloured dress and jacket, enlivened by blue glass beads.

And Gillian Perholt stared out of glassy eyes and heard her voice fail. She was far away and long ago – she was a pillar of salt, her voice echoed inside a glass box, a sad piping like a lost grasshopper in winter. She could move neither fingers nor lips, and in the body of the hall, behind the grey-scarved women, she saw a cavernous form, a huge, female form, with a veiled head bowed above emptiness and long slack-sinewed arms, hanging loosely around emptiness, and a draped, cowled garment ruffling over the windy vacuum of nothing, a thing banal in its conventional awfulness, and for that very reason appalling because it was there, to be seen, her eyes could distinguish each fold, could measure the red rims of those swollen eyes, could see the cracks in the stretched lips of that toothless, mirthless mouth, could see that it was many colours, and all of them grey, grey. The creature was flat-breasted and its withered skin was exposed above the emptiness, the windy hole that was its belly and womb.

This is what I am afraid of, thought Gillian Perholt, whose intelligence continued to work away, to think of ways to ascertain whether or not the thing was a product of hallucination or somehow out there on an unexpected wavelength.

And just as Orhan rose to come to her help, seeing her stare like Macbeth at the feast, she began to speak again, as though nothing had happened, and the audience sighed and sat back, ill at ease but courteous.

And what did Griselda do? asked Gillian Perholt. And what did Griselda say and what did she do? repeated Dr Perholt. First, all mazed, un-comprehending, she swooned. When she revived, she thanked her husband for having saved her chil-dren, and told her children that her father had cared for them tenderly – and she embraced both son and daughter, tightly, tightly, and still gripping them fell again into terrible unconsciousness, gripping so tightly that it was almost impossible for the bys-tanders to tear the children from her grasp. Chaucer does not say, the Clerk of Oxford does not say, that she was strangling them, but there is fear in his words, and in the power of her grip, all her stoppered and stunted energy forcing all three into unconsciousness, unknowing, absence from the finale so splendidly brought about by their lord and master.

But of course, she was revived, and again stripped of her old clothes, and dressed in cloth of gold and crowned with jewels and restored to her place at the feast. To begin again.

And I wish to say a few words, said Gillian Perholt, about the discomfort of this terrible tale. You might suppose it was one of that group of tales in which the father or king or lord tries to marry his daughter, after his wife's death, as the original Leontes tried to marry Perdita in the tale that precedes the *Winter's Tale*, the tale of a man seeking the return of spring and youth and fertility in ways inappropriate for human beings as opposed to grass and the flowers of the field. This pattern is painful but natural, this human error which tales hasten to punish and correct. But the peculiar horror of Patient Griselda does not lie in the psychological terror of incest or even of age. It lies in the narration of the story and Walter's relation to it. The story is terrible because Walter has assumed too many positions in the narration; he is hero, villain, destiny, God and narrator – there is no *play* in this tale, though the Clerk and Chaucer behind him try to vary its tone with reports of the people's contradictory feelings, and with the wry final comment on the happy marriage of Griselda's son, who

> fortunat was eek in mariage,
> Al putte he nat his wyf in greet assay.
> This world is nat so strong, it is no nay,
> As it hath been in olde tymes yoore.

And the commentator goes on to remark that the moral is *not* that wives should follow Griseldis in humility, for this would be impossible, unattainable, even if desired. The moral is that of Job, says the Clerk, according to Petrarch, that human beings must patiently bear what comes to them. And yet our own response is surely outrage – at what was done to Griselda – at what was taken from her, the best part of her life, what could not be restored – at the energy stopped off. For the stories of women's lives in fiction are the stories of stopped energies – the stories of Fanny Price, Lucy Snowe, even Gwendolen Harleth, are the stories of Griselda, and all come to that moment of strangling, willed oblivion.

Gillian Perholt looked up. The creature, the ghoul,

was gone. There was applause. She stepped down. Orhan, who was forthright and kind, asked if she felt unwell and she said that she had had a dizzy turn. She thought it was nothing to worry about. A momentary mild seizure. She would have liked to tell him about the apparition too, but was prevented. Her tongue lay like lead in her mouth, and the thing would not be spoken. What cannot be spoken continues its vigorous life in the veins, in the brain-cells, in the nerves. As a child she had known that if she could describe the grey men on the stairs, or the hag in the lavatory, they would vanish. But she could not. She imagined them lusciously and in terror and occasionally saw them, which was different.

Orhan's paper was the last in the conference. He was a born performer, and always had been, at least in Gillian's experience. She remembered a student production of *Hamlet* in which they had both taken part. Orhan had been Hamlet's father's ghost and had curdled everyone's blood with his deep-voiced rhetoric. His beard was now, as it had not been then, 'a sable silvered', and had now, as it had had then, an Elizabethan cut – though his face had sharpened from its youthful thoughtfulness and he now bore a resemblance, Gillian thought, to Bellini's portrait of Mehmet the Conqueror. She herself had been Gertrude, although she had wanted to be Ophelia, she had wanted to be beautiful and go passionately mad. She had been the Queen who could not see the spirit stalking her bedchamber: this came into her mind, with a renewed, now purely imaginary vision of the Hermione-Griselda ghoul, as she saw Orhan, tall, imposing, smiling in his beard, begin to speak of Scheherazade and the djinniyah.

'It has to be admitted,' said Orhan, 'that misogyny is a driving force of pre-modern story collections – perhaps especially of the frame stories – from *Katha Sarit Sagara*, *The Ocean of Story*, to the *Thousand and One Nights*, *Alf Layla wa-Layla*. Why this should be so has not, as far as I know, been fully explained, though there are reasons that could be put forward from social structures to depth psychology – the sad fact remains that women in these stories for the most part are portrayed as deceitful, unreliable, greedy, inordinate in their desires, unprincipled and simply dangerous, operating powerfully (apart from sorceresses and female ghouls and ogres) through the structures of powerlessness. What is peculiarly interesting about the *Thousand and One Nights* in terms of the subject of our conference, is the frame story, which begins with two kings driven to murderous despair by the treachery of women, yet has a powerful heroine-narrator, Scheherazade, who must daily save her own life from a blanket vicarious vengeance on all women by telling tales in the night, tales in the bed, in the bedchamber, to her innocent little sister – Scheherazade whose art is an endless beginning and delaying and ending and beginning and delaying and ending – a woman of infinite resource and sagacity,' said Orhan smiling, 'who is nevertheless using cunning and manipulation from a position of total powerlessness with the sword of her fate more or less in her bedchamber hanging like the sword of Damocles by a metaphorical thread, the thread of her narrative, with her shroud daily prepared for her the next morning. For King

Shahriyar, like Count Walter, has taken upon him-self to be husband and destiny, leaving only the storytelling element, the plotting, to his wife, which is enough. Enough to save her, enough to provide space for the engendering and birth of her children, whom she hides from her husband as Walter hid his from Griselda, enough to spin out her life until it becomes love and happy-ever-after, so to speak, as Griselda's does. For these tales are not psychological novels, are not concerned with states of mind or development of character, but bluntly with Fate, with Destiny, with what is pre-pared for human beings. And it has been excellently said by Pasolini the filmmaker that the tales in the *Thousand and One Nights* all end with the disappearance of destiny which 'sinks back into the somnolence of daily life'. But Scheherazade's own life could not sink back into somnolence until all the tales were told. So the dailiness of daily life is her end as it is Cinderella's and Snow-White's but not Mme Bovary's or Julien Sorel's who die but do not vanish into the afterlife of stories. But I am anti-cipating my argument, which, like my friend and

colleague Dr Perholt's argument, is about character and destiny and sex in the folk-tale, where
character is *not* destiny as Novalis said it was, but
something else is.

And first I shall speak of the lives of women in
the frame story, and then I shall briefly discuss the
story of Camaralzaman and Princess Budoor,
which is only half-told in the manuscripts of the
Nights . . .

Gillian Perholt sat behind the grey-scarved women
and watched Orhan's dark hooked face as he told of
the two kings and brothers Shahriyar and Shahzaman, and of how Shahzaman, setting out on a
journey to his brother went back home to bid his
wife farewell, found her in the arms of a kitchen
boy, slew them both immediately, and set out on
his journey consumed by despair and disgust.
These emotions were only relieved when he saw
from his brother's palace window the arrival in a
secret garden of his brother's wife and twenty slave
girls. Of these ten were white and ten black, and
the black cast off their robes revealing themselves
to be young males, who busily tupped the white

females, whilst the queen's black lover Mas'ud came out of a tree and did the same for her. This amused and relieved Shahzaman, who saw that his own fate was the universal fate, and was able to demonstrate to his brother, at first incredulous and then desperate with shame and wrath, that this was so. So the two kings, in disgust and despondency, left the court and their life at the same moment and set out on a pilgrimage in search of someone more unfortunate than themselves, poor cuckolds as they were.

Note, said Orhan, that at this time no one had attempted the lives of the queen and her black lover and the twenty lascivious slaves.

And what the two kings met was a djinn, who burst out of the sea like a swaying black pillar that touched the clouds, carrying on his head a great glass chest with four steel locks. And the two kings (like Mas'ud before them) took refuge in a tree. And the djinn laid himself down to sleep, as luck, or chance, or fate would have it, under that very tree, and opened the chest to release a beautiful woman – one he had carried away on her wedding night – on whose lap he laid his head and immediately began to snore. Whereupon the woman indicated to the two kings that she knew where they were, and would scream and reveal their presence to the djinn unless they immediately came down and satisfied her burning sexual need. The two kings found this difficult, in the circumstances, but were persuaded by threats of immediate betrayal and death to do their best. And when they had both made love to the djinn's stolen wife, as she lay with opened legs on the desert sand under the tree, she took from both of them their rings, which she put away in a small purse on her person, which already contained ninety-eight rings of varying fashions and materials. And she told the two kings with some complacency that they were all the rings of men with whom she had been able to deceive the djinn, despite being locked in a glass case with four steel locks, kept in the depths of the raging roaring sea. And the djinn, she explained, had tried in vain to keep her pure and chaste, not realising that nothing can prevent or alter what is predestined, and that when a woman desires something, nothing can stop her.

And the two kings concluded, after they were

well escaped, that the djinn was more unfortunate than they were, so they returned to the palace, put Shahriyar's wife and the twenty slaves to the sword, replaced the female slaves in the harem, and instituted the search for virgin brides who should all be put to death after one night 'to save King Shahriyar from the wickedness and cunning of women'. And this led to Scheherazade's resourceful plan to save countless other girls by substituting narrative attractions for those of inexperienced virginity, said Orhan, smiling in his beard, which took her a thousand and one nights. And in these frame stories, said Orhan, destiny for men is to lose dignity because of female rapacity and duplicity, and destiny for women is to be put to the sword on that account.

What interests me about the story of Prince Camaralzaman, said Orhan, is the activity of the djinn in bringing about a satisfactory adjustment to the normal human destiny in the recalcitrant prince. Camaralzaman was the beloved only son of Sultan Shahriman of Khalidan. He was the child of his father's old age, born of a virgin concubine with ample proportions, and he was very beautiful, like the moon, like new anemones in spring, like the children of angels. He was amiable but full of himself, and when his father urged him to marry to perpetuate his line, he cited the books of the wise, and their accounts of the wickedness and perfidy of women, as a reason for refraining. 'I would rather die than allow a woman to come near me,' said Prince Camaralzaman. 'Indeed,' he said grandly, 'I would not hesitate to kill myself if you wished to force me into marriage.' So his father left the topic for a year, during which Camaralzaman grew even more beautiful, and then asked again, and was told that the boy had done even more reading, which had simply convinced him that women were immoral, foolish and disgusting, and that death was preferable to dealing with them. And after another year, on the advice of his vizir, the king approached the prince formally in front of his court and was answered with insolence. So, on the advice of the vizir, the king confined his son to a ruined Roman tower, where he left him to fend for himself until he became more amenable.

Now, in the water-tank of the tower lived a djinniyah, a female djinn, who was a Believer, a servant of Suleyman, and full of energy. Djinns, as you may or may not know, are one of the three orders of created intelligences under Allah – the angels, formed of light, the djinns, formed of subtle fire, and man, created from the dust of the earth. There are three orders of djinns – flyers, walkers and divers; they are shape-shifters, and like human beings, divided into servants of God and servants of Iblis, the demon lord. The Koran often exhorts the djinns and men equally to repentance and belief, and there do exist legal structures governing the marriage and sexual relations of humans and djinns. They are creatures of this world, sometimes visible, sometimes invisible; they haunt bathrooms and lavatories, and they fly through the heavens. They have their own complex social system and hierarchies, into which I will not divagate. The djinniyah in question, Maimunah, was a flyer, and flew past the window of Camaralzaman's tower, where she saw the young man, beautiful as ever in his sleep, flew in and spent some time admiring him. Out again in the night sky she met another flying afrit, a lewd unbeliever called Dahnash who told her excitedly of a beautiful Chinese Princess, the lady Budoor, confined to her quarters by her old women, for fear she should stab herself, as she had sworn to do when threatened with a husband, asking, 'How shall my body, which can hardly bear the touch of silks, tolerate the rough approaches of a man?' And the two djinns began to dispute, circling on leathery wings in the middle air, as to which human creature, the male or the female, was the most beautiful. And the djinniyah commanded Dahnash to fetch the sleeping princess from China and lay her beside Prince Camaralzaman for comparison, which was performed, within an hour. The two genies, male and female, disputed hotly – and in formal verse – without coming to any conclusions as to the prize for beauty. So they summoned up a third being – a huge earth-spirit, with six horns, three forked tails, a hump, a limp, one immense and one pygmy arm, with claws and hooves, and monstrously lengthy masculinity. And this being performed a triumphal dance about the bed, and announced that the only way to test the relative power of these perfect beauties was to wake each in turn and see which showed the greater passion for the other, and the one who aroused the greatest lust would be the winner. So this was done; the prince was woken, swooning with desire and respect, and put to sleep with his desire unconsummated, and the princess was then woken, whose consuming need aroused power and reciprocating desire in the sleeping prince, and 'that happened which did happen'. And before I go on to recount and analyse the separation and madness of Camaralzaman and Budoor, the prince's long search, disguised as a geomancer, for his lost love, their marriage, their subsequent separation, owing to the theft of a talisman from the princess's drawers by a hawk, Princess Budoor's resourceful disguise as her husband, her wooing of a princess, her wooing of her own husband to what he thought were unnatural acts – before I tell all this I would like to comment on the presence of the djinns at this defloration of Budoor by Camaralzaman, their unseen delight in the human bodies, the strangeness of the apprehension of the secret consummation of first love as in fact the narrative contrivance of a group of bizarre and deeply involved onlookers, somewhere between gentlemen betting at a horse-race, entremetteurs, metteursen-scène or storytellers and gentlemen and ladies of the bedchamber. This moment of narrative, said Orhan, has always puzzled and pleased me because it is told from the point of view of these three magical beings, the prime instigator female, the subordinate ones male. What is the most private moment of choice in a human life – the loss of virginity, the mutual loss of virginity indeed, in total mutual satisfaction and bliss – takes place as a function of the desire and curiosity and competitive urgings of fire-creatures from sky and earth and cistern. Camaralzaman and Budoor – here also like Count Walter – have tried to preserve their freedom and their will, have rejected the opposite sex as ugly and disgusting and oppressive – and here in deepest dream they give way to their destiny which is conducted somewhere between comedy and sentimentality by this bizarre unseen trio – of whom the most redundant, from the point of view of the narrative, is also the largest, the most obtrusive, the most memorable, the horned, fork-tailed appallingly disproportioned solid earth-troll who capers in glee over the perfectly proportioned shapes of the two sleeping beauties. It is as though our dreams were watching us and directing our lives with external vigour whilst we simply enact their pleasures passively, in a swoon. Except that the djinns are more solid than dreams and have all sorts of other interests and preoccupations besides the young prince and princess . . .

The soldiers were writing busily; the scarved women stared ahead motionlessly, holding their heads high and proud. Gillian Perholt listened with pleasure to Orhan Rifat, who had gone on to talk more technically about the narrative imagination and its construction of reality in tales within tales within tales. She was tired; she had a slight temperature; the air of Ankara was full of fumes from brown coal, calling up her childhood days in a Yorkshire industrial city, where sulphur took her breath from her and kept her in bed with asthma, day after long day, reading fairy-tales and seeing the stories pass before her eyes. And they had gone to see *The Thief of Baghdad* when she was little; they had snuffed the sulphur as the enchanted horse swooped across the screen and the genie swelled from a speck to a cloud filling the whole sea-shore.

There had been an air-raid whilst they were in the cinema: the screen had flickered and jumped, and electric flashes had disturbed the magician's dark glare; small distant explosions had accompanied the princess's wanderings in the garden; they had all had to file out and hide in the cellars, she remembered, and she had wheezed, and imagined wings and fire in the evening air. What did I think my life was to be, then? Gillian Perholt asked herself, no longer listening to Orhan Rifat as he tried to define some boundary of credulity between fictive persons in the fictions of fictive persons in the fiction of real persons, in the reader and the writer. I had this idea of a woman I was going to be, and I think it was before I knew what sex was (she had been thinking with her body about the swooning delight of Camaralzaman and Princess Budoor) but I imagined I would be married, a married woman, I would have a veil and a wedding and a house and Someone – someone devoted, like the thief of Baghdad, and a dog. I wanted – but not by any stretch of the imagination to be a narratologist in Ankara, which is so much more interesting and surprising, she told herself, trying to listen to what Orhan Rifat was saying about thresholds and veils.

The next day she had half a day to herself and went to the Museum of Anatolian Civilisations which all her Turkish friends assured her she should not miss, and met an Ancient Mariner. The British Council car left her at the entrance to the museum, which is a modern building, cut into the hillside, made unobtrusively of wood and glass, a quiet, re-flective, thoughtful, elegant place, in which she had looked forward to being alone for an hour or two, and savouring her delightful redundancy. The ancient person in question emerged soundlessly from behind a pillar or statue and took her by the elbow. American? he said, and she replied indig-nantly, No, English, thus embarking willy-nilly on a conversation. I am the official guide, this person claimed. I fought with the English soldiers in Korea, good soldiers, the Turks and the English are both good soldiers. He was a heavy, squat, hairless man, with rolling folds between his cranium and his shoulders, and a polished gleam to his broad naked head, like marble. He wore a sheepskin jacket, a military medal, and a homemade-looking badge that said GUIDE. His forehead was low over his eye-sockets – he had neither brows nor lashes – and his wide mouth opened on a whitely gleaming row of large false teeth. I can show you everything, he said to Gillian Perholt, gripping her elbow, I know things you will never find out for yourself. She said neither yes nor no, but went down into the hall of the museum, with the muscular body of the ex-soldier shambling after her. Look, he said, as she stared into a reconstructed earth-dwelling, look how they lived in those days the first people, they dug holes like the animals, but they made them comfortable for themselves. Look here at the goddess. One day, think, they found themselves turning the bits of clay in their hands, and they saw a head and a body, see, in the clay, they saw a leg and an arm, they pushed a bit and pinched bit here and there and there She was, look at her, the little fat woman. They loved fat, it meant strength and good prospects of children and living through the winter, to those naked people, they were probably thin and half-starved with hunting and hiding in holes, so they made her fat, fat, fat was life to them.

And who knows why they made the first little woman, a doll, an image, a little offering to the goddess, to propitiate her – what came first, the doll or the goddess we cannot know – but we *think* they worshipped her, the fat woman, we think they thought everything came out of her hole, as they came out of their underground houses, as the plants and trees come out in the spring after the dark. Look at her here, here she is very old, 8,000 years, 9,000 years before your Christian time-counting, here she is only the essential, a head, and arms, and legs and lovely fat belly, breasts to feed, no need even for hands or feet, here, see no face. Look at her, made out of the dust of the earth by human fingers so old, so old you can't really imagine.

And Gillian Perholt looked at the little fat dolls with their bellies and breasts, and pulled in her stomach muscles, and felt the fear of death in the muscles of her heart, thinking of these centuries'-old fingers fashioning flesh of clay.

And later, he said, guiding her from figure to figure, she became powerful, she became the god-dess in the lion throne, see here she sits, she is the ruler of the world now, she sits in her throne with her arms on the lion-heads, and see there, the head of the child coming out between her legs, see how well those old people knew how to show the little skull of the baby as it turns to be born.

There were rows of the little baked figurines; all generically related, all different also. The woman in rolls of fat on the squat throne, crowned with a circlet of clay, and the arms of the throne were standing lions and her buttocks protruded behind her, and her breasts fell heavy and splayed, and her emptying belly sagged realistically between her huge fat knees. She was one with her throne, the power of the flesh. Her hands were lion-heads, her head bald as the ancient soldier's and square down the back of the fat neck as his was.

We don't like our girls fat now, said the ancient one, regretfully. We like them to look like young boys, the boys out of the Greek gymnasium round the corner. Look at her, though, you can see how powerful she was, how they touched her power, scratching the shape into her breasts there, full of goodness they thought and hoped.

Gillian Perholt did not look at the old soldier

whose voice was full of passion; she had not exactly consented to his accompanying narrative, and
the upper layer of her consciousness was full of
embarrassed calculations about how much Turkish
cash she was carrying and how that would convert
into pounds sterling, and how much such a guide
might require at the end of his tale, if she could not
shed him. So they trod on, one behind the other,
she never turning her head or meeting his eye, and
he never ceasing to speak into her ear, into the back
of her studious head, as he darted from glass case to
glass case, manoeuvring his bulk lightly and
silently, as though shod with felt. And in the cases
the clay women were replaced by metal stags and
sun-discs, and the tales behind her were tales of
kings and armies, of sacrifice and slaughter, of
bride-sacrifice and sun-offerings, and she was
helplessly complicit, for here was the best, the most
assured raconteur she could hope to meet. She
knew nothing of the Hittites or the Mesopotamians
or the Babylonians or the Sumerians, and not much
of the Egyptians and the Romans in this context,
but the soldier did, and made a whole wedding
from a two-spouted wine-jar in the form of ducks,

or from a necklace of silver and turquoise, and a centuries-old pot of kohl he made a nervous bride, looking in a bronze mirror – his whisper called up her black hair, her huge eyes, her hand steadying the brush, her maid, her dress of pleated linen. He talked too, between centuries and between cases, of the efficiency of the British and Turkish soldiers fighting side by side on the Korean hillsides, and Gillian remembered her husband saying that the Turks' punishments for pilfering and desertion had been so dreadful that they were bothered by neither. And she thought of Orhan, saying, 'People who think of Turks think of killing and lasciviousness, which is sad, for we are complicated and have many natures. Including a certain ferocity. And a certain pleasure in good living.'

The lions of the desert were death to the peoples of Anatolia, said the old guide, as they neared the end of their journey, which had begun with the earth-dwellers and moved through the civilisations that built the sun-baked ziggurats, towards the lion-gates of Nineveh and Assyria. That old goddess, she sat on the lion-throne, the lions were a part of her power, she was the earth and the lions.

And later the kings and the warriors tamed the lions and took on their strength, wore their skins and made statues of them as guardians against the wild. Here are the Persian lions, the word is Aslan, they are strength and death, you can walk through that carved lion-gate into the world of the dead, as Gilgamesh did in search of Enkidu his friend who was dead. Do you know the story of Gilgamesh, the old man asked the woman, as they went through the lion gates together, she always in front and with averted eyes. The museum had arranged various real carved walls and gates into imaginary passages and courtyards, like a minor maze in a cool light. They were now, in the late afternoon, the only two people in the museum, and the old soldier's voice was hushed, out of awe perhaps, of the works of the dead, out of respect perhaps, for the silence of the place, where the glass cases gleamed in the shadows.

See here, he said, with momentary excitement, see here is the story of Gilgamesh carved in stone if you know how to read it. See here is the hero clothed in skins and here is his friend the wild man with his club – here is their meeting, here they wrestle and make friends on the threshold of the king's palace. Do you know Enkidu? He was huge and hairy, he lived with the beasts in the woods and fields, he helped them escape the trappers and hunters. But the trappers asked Gilgamesh the king to send a woman, a whore, who tempted Enkidu to leave the world of the gazelles and the herds and come to the king, who fought him and loved him. And they were inseparable, and together they killed the giant Humbaba – tricked and killed him in the forest. They trick and kill him, they are young and strong, there is nothing they cannot do. But then Gilgamesh's youth and strength attract the attention of the goddess Ishtar – she was the goddess of Love, and also of War – she is the same goddess you know, ma'am, as Cybele and Astarte – and when the Romans came with their Diana she was the same goddess – terrible and beautiful – whose temples were surrounded by whores – holy whores – whose desires could not be denied. And Ishtar wanted to marry Gilgamesh but he repelled her – he thought she would trick him and destroy him, and he made the mistake of telling her so, telling her he didn't want her, he wanted to remain free

– for she had destroyed Tammuz, he said, whom the women wailed for, and she had turned shepherds into wolves and rejected lovers into blind moles, and she had destroyed the lions in pits and the horses in battle, although she loved their fierceness. And this made Ishtar angry – and she sent a great bull from heaven to destroy the kingdom, but the heroes killed the bull – see here in the stone they drive their sword behind his horns – and Enkidu ripped off the bull's thigh and threw it in the face of Ishtar. And she called the temple whores to weep for the bull and decided Enkidu must die. See here, he lies sick on his bed and dreams of death. For young men, you know, they do not know death, or they think of it as a lion or a bull to be wrestled and conquered. But sick men know death, and Enkidu dreamed of His coming – a bird-man with a ghoul-face and claws and feathers – for the loathsome picture of death, you see, is from the vulture – and Enkidu dreamed that this Death was smothering him and turning him into the bird-man and that he was going to the Palace of the gods of the underworld – and there, Enkidu saw in his dream, there was no light at all and no joy and the people ate dust and fed on clay. There is a goddess down there too – here she is – Ereshkigal the Queen of the underworld. And both Gilgamesh and Enkidu wept at this dream – it terrified them – it took away all their strength – and then Enkidu died, in terrible pain, and Gilgamesh could not be comforted. He would not accept that his friend was gone and would never come back. He was young and strong, he would not accept that there was death walking in the world. Young men are like that, you know, it's a truth – they think they can defy what's coming because their blood is hot and their bodies are strong.

And Gilgamesh remembered his ancestor, Uta-Napishtim who was the only man who had survived when the earth was flooded; they said he lived in the underworld and had the secret of living forever. So Gilgamesh travelled on and travelled on, and came to a mountain called Mashu, and at the mountain's gate were the man-scorpions, demons you know, like dragons. We can pretend that this gate is the gate of the underworld – the Sumerian people, the Babylonian people, they made great solid gates to their buildings and built guardians into the gates. See here are lions, and here, at this gate, are genies – you say genies? – yes, genies, – there were good genies and bad genies in Babylon, they were called *utukku* and some were good and some were evil – the good ones were like these guardians here who are bulls with wings and wise faces of men – they are called *shedu* or *lamassu* – they stand here as guardians, but they could take other shapes, they walked invisibly behind men in the streets; every one had his genie, some people say, and they protected them – there is an old saying 'he who has no genie when he walks in the streets wears a headache like a garment'. That's interesting, don't you think?

Gillian Perholt nodded. She had a headache herself – she had had a kind of penumbral headache, accompanied by occasional stabs from invisible stilettos or ice-splinters since she had seen the Griselda-ghoul, and everything shimmered a little, with a grey shimmer, in the space between the gate and the narratives carved in relief on the stone tablets. The old soldier had become more and more animated, and now began to act out Gilgamesh's

arrival at the gates of Mount Meshu, almost dancing like a bear, approaching, stepping back, staring
up, skipping briskly from the courtyard to the
space between the gateposts, raising his fingers to
his bald skull for horns and answering himself in
the person of the scorpion-men. (These are *good*
genies, ma'am, said the old soldier parenthetically.
The scorpion-men might have been dangerous
ones, *edimmu* or worse, *arallu*, who came out of the
underworld and caused pestilence, they sprang
from the goddess's bile, you must imagine terrifying scorpion-men in the place of these bulls with
wings.) They say, Why have you come? And Gilgamesh says 'For Enkidu my friend. And to see my
father Uta-Napishtim among the gods.' And they
say 'No man born of woman has gone into the
mountain; it is very deep; there is no light and the
heart is oppressed with darkness. Oppressed with
darkness.' He skipped out again and strode resolutely in, as Gilgamesh. She thought, he is a
descendant of the ashiks of whom I have read, who
dressed in a uniform of skins, and wore a skin hat
and carried a club or a sword as a professional prop.
They made shadows with their clubs on café walls

and in market squares. The old soldier's shadow mopped and mowed amongst the carved *utukku*: he was Gilgamesh annihilated in the dark; he came out into the light and became Siduri, the woman of the vine, in the garden at the edge of the sea with golden bowl and golden vats of wind; he became Urshanabi the ferryman of the Ocean, disturbed at the presence of one who wore skins and ate flesh, in the other world. He was, Gillian Perholt thought suddenly, related to Karagöz and Hacivat, the comic heroes and animators of the Turkish shadow-puppets, who fought both demons from the underworld and fat capitalists. Orhan Rifat was a skilled puppeteer: he had a leather case full of the little figures whom he could bring to life against a sheet hung on a frame, against a white wall.

'And Uta-Napishtim,' said the Ancient Mariner, sitting down suddenly on a stone lion, and fixing Gillian Perholt with his eye, 'Uta-Napishtim told Gilgamesh that there was a plant, a flower, that grew under the water. It was a flower with a sharp thorn that would wound his hands – but if he could win it he would have his lost youth again. So Gilgamesh tied heavy stones to his feet and sank into

the deep water and walked in the seabed, and came
to the plant which did prick him, but he grasped it
and brought it up again into the light. And Gilgamesh set out again with Urshanabi the ferryman to
take the flower back to the old men of his city,
Uruk, to bring back their lost youths. And when
they had travelled on and on, said the Ancient
Mariner, weaving his way between the ancient
monuments in his shuffling dance, he came to a
deep well of cool water, and he bathed in it, and re-
freshed himself. But deep in the pool there was a
snake, and this snake sensed the sweetness of the
flower. So it rose up through the water, and
snatched the flower, and ate it. And then it cast off
its skin, in the water, and swam down again, out of
sight. And Gilgamesh sat down and wept, his tears
ran down his face, and he said to Urshanabi the
ferryman, "Was it for this that I worked so hard, is
it for this that I forced out my heart's blood? For
myself I have gained nothing – I don't have it, a
beast out of the earth has it now. I found a sign and
I have lost it." '

The heavy bald head turned towards Gillian
Perholt and the lashless eyelids slid blindly down

over the eyeballs for a moment in what seemed to be exhaustion. The thick hands fumbled at the pockets of the fleece-lined jacket for a moment, as though the fingers were those of Gilgamesh, searching for what he had lost. And Gillian's inner eye was full of the empty snakeskin, a papery shadowy form of a snake which she saw floating at the rim of the well into which the muscular snake had vigorously vanished.

'What does it mean, my lady?' asked the old man. 'It means that Gilgamesh must die now – he has seen that he could grasp the thorn and the flower and live forever – but the snake took it just by chance, not to hurt him, but because it liked the sweetness. It is so sad to hold the sign and lose it, it is a sad story – because in most stories where you go to find something you bring it back after your struggles, I think, but here the beast, the creature, just took it, just by chance, after all the effort. They were a sad people, ma'am, very sad. Death hung over them.'

When they came out into the light of day she gave him what Turkish money she had, which he looked over, counted, and put in his pocket. She could not tell if he thought it too little or too much: the folds of his bald head wrinkled as he considered it. The British Council driver was waiting with the car; she walked towards him. When she turned to say goodbye to the Mariner, he was no longer to be seen.

Turks are good at parties. The party in Izmir was made up of Orhan's friends – scholars and writers, journalists and students. 'Smyrna', said Orhan, as they drove into the town, holding their noses as they went along the harbour-front with its stench of excrement, 'Smyrna of the merchants', as they looked up at the quiet town on its conical hill. 'Smyrna where we like to think Homer was born, the place most people agree he was probably born.'

It was spring, the air was light and full of new sunshine. They ate stuffed peppers and vineleaves, kebabs and smoky aubergines in little restaurants; they made excursions and ate roasted fishes at a trestle table set by a tiny harbour, looking at fishing boats that seemed timeless, named for the stars and the moon. They told each other stories. Orhan told of his tragi-comic battle with the official powers over his beard, which he had been required to shave before he was allowed to teach. A beard in modern Turkey is symbolic of religion or Marxism, neither acceptable. He had shaved his beard temporarily but now it flourished anew, like mown grass, Orhan said, even thicker and more luxuriant. The conversation moved to poets and politics: the exile of Halicarnassus, the imprisonment of the great Nazim Hikmet. Orhan recited Hikmet's poem, 'Weeping Willow', with its fallen rider and the drumming beat of the hooves of the red horsemen, vanishing at the gallop. And Leyla Serin recited Faruk Nafiz Çamlibel's *Göksu*, with its own weeping willow.

> Whenever my heart would wander in Göksu
> The garden in my dreams falls on the wood.
> At dusk the roses seem a distant veil
> The phantom willow boughs a cloak and hood.
>
> Bulbuls and hoopoes of a bygone age
> Retell their time-old ballads in the dark
> The blue reflecting waters hear and show
> The passing of Nedim with six-oared barque . . .

And Gillian told the story of her encounter with the old soldier in the Anatolian museum. 'Maybe he was a djinn,' said Orhan. 'A djinn in Turkish is spelled CIN and you can tell one, if you meet it, in its human form, because it is naked and hairless. They can take many forms but their human form is hairless.'

'He had a hairy coat,' said Gillian, 'but he was hairless. His skin was ivory-yellow, beeswax colour, and he had no hair anywhere.'

'Certainly a djinn,' said Orhan.

'In that case,' said the young Attila, who had spoken on 'Bajazet in the Harem', 'how do you explain the Queen of Sheba?'

'What should I explain about her?' said Orhan.

'Well,' said Attila, 'in Islamic tradition, Solomon travelled from Mecca to Sheba to see this queen, who was said to have hairy legs like a donkey because she was the daughter of a djinn. So Solomon asked her to marry him, and to please him she used various unguents and herbs to render her legs as smooth as a baby's skin . . .'

'*Autres pays, autres moeurs,*' said Leyla Doruk. 'You can't pin down djinns. As for Dr Perholt's *naqqual*, he seems to be related to the earth-spirit in the story of Camaralzaman, don't you think so?'

They went also on an excursion to Ephesus. This is a white city risen, in part, from the dead: you can walk along a marble street where St Paul must have walked; columns and porticoes, the shell of an elegant library, temples and caryatids are again upright in the spring sun. The young Attila frowned as they paced past the temple façades and said they made him shiver: Gillian thought he was thinking of the death of nations, but it turned out that he was thinking of something more primitive and more immediate, of earthquakes. And when he said that, Gillian looked at the broken stones with fear too.

In the museum are two statues of the Artemis of Ephesus, whose temple, the Artemision, was one of the Seven Wonders of the Ancient World, rediscovered in the nineteenth century by a dogged and inspired English engineer, John Turtle Wood. The colossal Artemis is more austere, and like Cybele, the Magna Mater, turret-crowned, with a temple on her head, under whose arches sit winged sphinxes.

Her body is a rising pillar: her haunches can be seen within its form but she wears like a skirt the beasts of the field, the wood, the heavens, all geometrically arranged in quadrangles between carved stone ropes, in twos and threes: bulls, rams, antelopes, winged bulls, flying sphinxes with women's breasts and lion-heads, winged men and huge hieratic bees, for the bee is her symbol, and the symbol of Ephesus. She is garlanded with flowers and fruit, all part of the stone of which she is made: lions crouch in the crook of her arm (her hands are lost) and her headdress or veil is made of ranks of winged bulls, like the genies at the gates in the Ankara museum. And before her she carries, as a date-palm carries dates, her triple row of full breasts, seven, eight, eight, fecundity in stone. The lesser Artemis, whom the Turks call Güzel Artemis and the French La Belle Artémis, stands in front of a brick wall and has a less Egyptian, more oriental, faintly smiling face. She too wears the beasts of earth and air like a garment, bulls and antelopes, winged bulls and sphinxes, with the lions couched below the rows of pendent breasts in their shadow. Her headdress too is woven of winged bulls, though her temple crown is lost. But she has her feet, which are side by side inside a reptilian frill or scallop or serpent-tail, and at these feet are honeycombed beehives. Her eyes are wide, and heavy-lidded: she looks out of the stone.

The party admired the goddess. Orhan bowed to her, and Leyla Doruk and Leyla Serin explained her cult to Gillian Perholt, how she was certainly really a much older goddess than the Greek Artemis or the Roman Diana, an Asian earth-goddess, Cybele, Astarte, Ishtar, whose temple was served by virgins and temple prostitutes, who combined extremes of abundant life and fierce slaughter, whose male priests castrated themselves in a frenzy of devotion, like those dying gods, Tammuz, Attis, Adonis, with whose blood the rivers ran red to the sea. The women wept for these dying divinities, said Leyla Serin. It was believed that Coleridge found his wonderful phrase, 'woman wailing for her demon lover', in descriptions of these ritual mournings.

There was a priest, said Leyla Doruk, the Megabyxus; that is a Persian word, and it means set free by God. He was probably a foreign eunuch. There were three priestesses – the Virgin Priestess, the Novice, the Future Priestess, and the Old Priestess who taught the young ones. The priestesses were called Melissae, which is bees. And there were priests called the Acrobatae who walked on tiptoe, and priests called the Essenes, another non-Greek word, Essen means king bee – the Greeks didn't know that the queen bee is a queen, but we know now. . . .

'Her breasts are frightening,' said Gillian Perholt. 'Like Medusa's snakes, too much, but an orderly too much.'

'Some people now say the breasts are not breasts but eggs,' said Attila. 'Symbols of rebirth.'

'They *have* to be breasts,' said Gillian Perholt. 'You cannot see this figure and not read those forms as breasts.'

'Some say,' said Leyla Doruk, smiling, 'that they were bulls' testicles, sacrificed to her, you know, hung round her in her honour, as the – the castrated priests' – parts – once were.'

They were ripe and full and stony.

'They are metaphors,' said Orhan. 'They are

many things at once, as the sphinxes and winged bulls are many things at once.'

'You admire her, our goddess,' said Leyla Doruk.

She is not yours, thought Gillian. You are late-comers. She is older and stronger. Then she thought: but she is more yours than mine, all the same. The brick wall behind the Güzel Artemis, the beautiful Artemis, was hung with plastic ivy, fading creamy in the sunlight.

The two Leylas stood with Gillian Perholt in front of the Güzel Artemis and each took her by one arm, laughing.

'Now, Dr Perholt,' said Leyla Osman, 'you must make a wish. For here, if you stand between two people with the same name, and wish, it will come true.'

Leyla Doruk was large and flowing; Leyla Serin was small and bird-like. Both had large dark eyes and lovely skins. They made Gillian Perholt feel hot, anglo-saxon, padded and clumsy. She was used to ignoring these feelings. She said, laughing,

'I am enough of a narratologist to know that no

good ever comes of making wishes. They have a habit of twisting the wishers to their own ends.'

'Only foolish wishes,' said Leyla Serin. 'Only the uninstructed, who don't think.'

'Like the peasant who saved a magic bird which gave him three wishes, and he wished for a string of sausages in his pan, and they were there, and his wife said that that was a foolish wish, a stupid wish, a string of sausages with the whole world to wish for, and he was so mad at her, he wished the sausages would stick to her nose, and they did, and that was two wishes, and he had to use the third on detaching them.'

For a moment this fictive Nordic peasant's wife, decorated with sausage strings, was imaginatively present also before the goddess with her rows of dangling breasts. Everyone laughed. Wish, Gillian, said Orhan. You are quite intelligent enough not to wish for anything silly.

'In England,' said Gillian, 'when we wish, when we cut our birthday-cakes, we scream out loud, to turn away the knife, I suppose.'

'You may scream if you want to,' said Leyla Serin.

'I am not in England,' said Gillian Perholt. 'And it is not my birthday. So I shall not scream, I shall concentrate on being intelligent, as Orhan has commanded.'

She closed her eyes, and concentrated, and wished, seeing the red light inside her eyelids, as so often before, hearing a faint drumming of blood in her ears. She made a precise and careful wish to be asked to give the keynote address at the Toronto Conference of narratologists in the Fall and added a wish for a first-class air-fare and a hotel with a swimming-pool, as a kind of wishing-package, she explained to the blood thrumming in her eyes and ears, and opened the eyes again, and shook her head before the smiling Artemis. Everyone laughed. You looked so serious, they said, squeezing her arms before they let go, and laughing.

They walked through old-new Ephesus and came to the theatre. Orhan stood against the ruined stage and said something incantatory in Turkish which he then explained to Gillian was Dionysus' first speech, his terrible, smiling, threatening speech at the beginning of *The Bacchae*. He then threw one arm over his shoulder and became cloaked and tall and stiffly striding where he had been supple and smiling and eastern. 'Listen, Gillian,' he said:

'I could a tale unfold whose lightest word
Would harrow up thy soul, freeze thy young blood
Make thy two eyes like stars, start from their spheres,
Thy knotted and combined locks to part.
And each particular hair to stand on end
Like quills upon the fretful porpentine.
But this eternal blazon must not be
To ears of flesh and blood.'

'Angels and ministers of grace defend us,' said Gillian, laughing, remembering the young Orhan stalking the English student stage; thinking too of Mehmet the Conqueror, as Bellini saw him, eloquent, watchful and dangerous.

'I was good,' said Orhan, 'in those days. It was his part. Shakespeare himself played the Ghost. Did you know that, Attila? When you speak these words you speak the words he spoke.'

'Not on this stage,' said Attila.

'Now,' said Orhan. 'Now it is here.'

Angels had made Gillian think of St Paul. Angels

had sprung open St Paul's prison in Ephesus. She had sat in Sunday school, hearing a fly buzzing against a smeared high window in the vestry and had hated the stories of St Paul and the other apostles because they were true, they were told to her as true stories, and this somehow stopped off some essential imaginative involvement with them, probably because she didn't believe them, if required to believe they were true. She was Hamlet and his father and Shakespeare: she saw Milton's snake and the miraculous flying horse of the Thief of Baghdad, but St Paul's angels rested under suspicion of being made-up because she had been told they were special because *true*. St Paul had come here to Ephesus to tell the people here that Artemis was not true, was not real, because she was a god made with hands. He had stood here, precisely here, in this theatre, she understood slowly; this real man, a provincial interloper with a message, had stood here, where she now stood. She found this hard to believe because St Paul had always seemed to her so cardboard, compared, when she met them later, to Dionysus, to Achilles, to Priam. But he had come here with his wrath against hand-made gods. He had changed the world. He had been a persecutor and had been blinded by light on the road to Damascus (for that moment he was not cardboard, he was consumed by light) and had set out to preach the new god, whom he had not, in his human form, known. In Ephesus he had caused 'no small stir'. His preaching had angered Demetrius, a silversmith, who made silver shrines for the goddess. And Demetrius stirred up the people of Ephesus against the saint, who claimed 'they be no gods which are made with hands' and told them that the foreign preacher would not only set their craft at naught but also 'the temple of the great goddess Diana should be despised, and her magnificence should be destroyed, whom all Asia and the world worshippeth.'

'And when they heard these sayings, they were full of wrath, and cried out, saying, Great is Diana of the Ephesians.

'And the whole city was filled with confusion: and having caught Gaius and Artistarchus, men of Macedonia, Paul's companions in travel, they rushed with one accord into the theatre.

'And there for two hours they continued to cry Great is Diana of the Ephesians.'

And because of the uproar, which was calmed by the town clerk, Paul left the city of Ephesus and set off for Macedonia.

So the bristling apostle was beaten by commerce and the power of the goddess.

'You know,' said Leyla Doruk, 'that your Virgin Mary came and died here. It is not certain, as it is not certain that Homer was born in Izmir, but it is said to be so, and her house was discovered because of a sick German lady in the nineteenth century who saw it in visions, the house and the hills, and when they came to look it was there, or so they say. We call it Panaya Kapulu, there is a Christian church too. She came with John, they say, and died here.'

At a nightclub in Istanbul once, Gillian had been shocked, without quite knowing why, to find one of those vacant, sweetly pink and blue church Virgins, life-size, standing as part of the decorations, part hat-stand, part dumb-waitress, as you might

find a many-handed Hindu deity or a plaster Venus
in an equivalent occidental club. Now suddenly,
she saw a real bewildered old woman, a woman
with a shrivelled womb and empty eyes, a woman
whose son had been cruelly and very slowly
slaughtered before her eyes, shuffling through the
streets of Ephesus, waiting quietly for death until it
came. And then, afterwards, this old woman, this
real dead old woman had in part become the
mother goddess, the Syria Dea, the crowned
Queen. She was suddenly aware of every inch of
her own slack and dying skin. She thought of the
stone eyes of the goddess, of her dangerous dignity, of her ambiguous plump breasts, dead balls,
intact eggs, wreathed round her in triumph and
understood that real-unreal was not the point, that
the goddess was still, and always had been, and in
the foreseeable future would be more alive, more
energetic, infinitely more powerful than she herself, Gillian Perholt, that she would stand here
before her children, and Orhan's children, and their
children's children and smile, when they themselves were scattered atomies.

And when she thought this, standing amongst a

group of smiling friends in the centre of the theatre at Ephesus, she experienced again the strange stoppage of her own life that had come with the vision of Patient Griselda. She put out a hand to Orhan and could move no more; and it seemed that she was in a huge buzzing dark cloud, sparking with flashes of fire, and she could smell flowers, and her own blood, and she could hear rushing and humming in her veins, but she could not move a nerve or a muscle. And after a moment, a kind of liquid sob rose in her throat, and Orhan saw the state she was in, and put an arm round her shoulder, and steadied her, until she came to herself.

In the aeroplane on the way back to Istanbul, Orhan said to Gillian:

'Forgive me, are you quite well?'

'Never better,' said Gillian, which was in many senses true. But she knew she must answer him. 'I do truly mean, I feel more alive now than ever before. But lately I've had a sense of my fate – my death, that is – waiting for me, manifesting itself from time to time, to remind me it's there. It isn't a battle. I don't fight it off. It takes charge for a moment or two, and then lets go again, and steps back. The more alive I am, the more suddenly it comes.'

'Should you see a doctor?'

'When I am so *well*, Orhan?'

'I am delighted to see you so well,' said Orhan. The plane came down into Istanbul and the passengers began a decorous and delightful clapping, applause perhaps for the pilot's skill, applause perhaps for another successful evasion of fate.

In Istanbul Orhan Rifat, a very happily married man, returned to his family, and Gillian Perholt settled in for a few days in the Peri Palas Hotel, which was not the famous Pera Palas, in the old European city across the Golden Horn, but a new hotel, of the kind Gillian liked best, combining large hard beds, elegant mirrored bathrooms, lifts and a swimming pool with local forms and patterns – tiled fountains, Turkish tiles with pinks and cornflowers in the bathrooms, carpets woven with abundant silky flowers in the small sitting rooms and writing rooms. It was constructed around a beehive of inner courtyards, with balconies rising one above the other, and silky translucent white-gold curtains behind functional double-glazed balcony doors. Gillian had developed a late passion for swimming. Flying distorts the human body – the middle-aged female body perhaps particularly – the belly balloons, the ankles become cushions of flesh and air, the knees round into puffballs, toes and fingers are swollen and shiny. Gillian had learned never to look in the mirror on arrival, for what stared out at her was a fleshy monster. She had learned to hurry to the pool, however little she felt inclined to exert herself, for what air pressure inflates, water pressure delicately makes weightless and vanishing. The pool at the Peri Palas was empty on the day of Gillian's arrival, and very satisfactory, if small. It was underground, a large tank, tiled in a dark emerald green, lit from within by gold-rimmed lamps, and the walls of its cavern were tiled with blue and green tiles covered with chrysanthemums and carnations, edged with gold mosaic, glinting and gleaming in the golden light. Oh the bliss, said Gillian to herself as she extended her sad body along the green rolls of swaying liquid and felt it vanish, felt her blood and nerves become pure energy, moved forward with a ripple like a swimming serpent. Little waves of her own making lapped her chin in this secret cistern; her ears were full of the soft whisper and plash of water, her eyes were wide upon green and green, woven with networks of swaying golden light. She basked, she rolled, she flickered ankles and wrists, she turned on her back and let her hair fan on the glassy curves. The nerves unknotted, the heart and lungs settled and pumped, the body was alive and joyful.

When Orhan took her to Topkapı her body was still comfortable from the swimming, which her skin remembered as the two of them looked down from the Sultan's upper window on the great dark tank under cedars where once the women of the harem swam together in the sun. In the harem too, was the Sultan's bath, a quite different affair, a central box inside a series of carved boxes and cupboards inside the quarters of the Valide Sultan, his mother, where his nakedness could be guarded by many watchful eyes from assassin's knives. Here too, as in Ephesus, Gillian Perholt struggled with the passions of real stories. Here in the cages the sons of the sultans had waited for the eunuchs with the silken cords that would end their lives and make the throne safe for the chosen one. Here intriguing or unsatisfactory women had been caught and tied in sacks and drowned; here captives, or unsatisfactory servants, had been beheaded for a whim of an absolute ruler. How did they live with such fear? She said to Orhan:

'It is as you said of Shahriyar and I said of Walter – there must be a wonderful pleasure for some people in being other people's fates and destinies. Perhaps it gave them the illusion that their own fates too were in their own hands – '

'Perhaps,' said Orhan. 'Perhaps life mattered less to them, their own or anyone else's.'

'Do you really think they thought that?'

'No,' said Orhan, looking round the empty maze of hidden rooms and secret places. 'No, not really. We like to say that. They believed in a future life. We can't imagine that.'

Showing her round Istanbul, nevertheless, Orhan became more Turkish. Before the great gold throne of Murat III studded with emeralds, and cushioned in gold and white silk, he said,

'We were a nomadic people. We came over the steppes from Mongolia, from China. Our thrones are portable treasures, our throne-rooms resemble tents, we put our skill into small things, daggers and bowls and cups.' She remembered the rhythms of his recitation of the poem of the red horsemen.

In the Haghia Sophia she had her third encounter with Fate, or with something. Haghia Sophia is a confusing place, echoing and empty, hugely domed and architecturally uncertain, despite its vast and imposing space: it has been church and mosque and modern museum; it has minarets and patches, ghosts, of ruined gold mosaics of Byzantine emperors and the Christian mother and child. The emperor Justinian built it from eclectic materials, collecting pillars and ornaments from temples in Greece and Egypt, including pillars from the temple of the Goddess in Ephesus. It could feel – Gillian had expected it to feel – like a meeting-place of cultures, of east and west, the Christian Church and Islam, but it did not. It felt like an empty exhausted barn, exhausted by battle and pillage and religious rage. Whatever had been there had gone, had fled long ago, Gillian felt, and Orhan too showed no emotion, but returned to his European academic self, pointing out the meanings of the mosaics and talking of his own new thoughts about the absurdities of the theories of Marcuse which had been all the rage in the sixties, when they began to teach. 'There is a curious pillar here,' he said vaguely, 'somewhere or other, with a hole of some sort, where people wish, you might like to see that, if I can find it. The stone is worn away by people touching it, I forget what it does, but you might like to see it.'

'It doesn't matter,' said Gillian.

'They put a brass casing round the magic stone to preserve it,' said Orhan. 'But the pilgrims have worn it away, they have eaten into the pillar just with touching, through the brass and the stone. Now where is it, I should be able to find it. It is like wearing away with waterdrops, wearing away with faith, I find that quite interesting, I wish I could remember what it *does*.'

When they came to it, there was a family already

clustered round it, a Pakistani father and his wife and two daughters, richly beautiful in saris, one pink and gold, one peacock and flame, one blue and silver. They had found the pillar with the hole and its brass casing, and the three women were clustered round it, stroking, putting their hands in and out, chattering like subdued birds. The father, dignified in his black coat, approached Orhan, and asked if he spoke English. Orhan said yes, and was asked to help translate an account of the pillar from a French-Turkish guidebook.

Whilst he did this, the three women, in their fluttering silk, turned laughing to Gillian Perholt, and stretched out three soft hands with gold bangles on their wrists, pulling her by her sleeve, by her hand, towards the pillar, laughing softly. They patted Dr Perholt's shoulders, they put arms around her and pushed and pulled, smiling and laughing, they took her hand in theirs with strong, wiry grips and inserted it into the hole, showing her in mime what she must do, turn her hand in the hole, touching the inside rim, round, round, round, three times. She pulled back instinctively, out of an English hygienic horror of something so much touched by so many, and out of a more primitive fear, of something clammy, and moist, and nasty in the dark inside. But the women insisted; they were surprisingly forceful. There was liquid of some kind in there, some pool of something in the stem of the pillar. Dr Perholt's skin crawled and the women laughed, and Orhan recited the story of the pillar in English to the other man. Apparently, he said, it had been touched by St Gregory Thaumaturge, the Miracle-Worker, he had put his power into it. The water inside the pillar was efficacious for diseases of vision and for fertility. The women laughed more loudly, clustering round Dr Perholt. The father told Orhan how he had made pilgrimage to all the holy shrines of Islam; he had travelled far and seen much. He supposed Orhan too, had made pilgrimages. Orhan nodded, grave and non-committal; he was interested. The West was evil, said the respectable black-coated pilgrim. Evil, decadent, and sliding into darkness. But power was arising. There would be a jihad. True religion would bring the cleansing sword and destroy the filth and greed and corruption of the dying West, and a religious world would be established in its

175

ashes; these things were not only possible, they were already happening. The seeds were sown, the sparks were set, the field of spears would spring up, the fire would consume. This was what he said, this paterfamilias, standing in Haghia Sophia whose stones had run with blood, whose cavernous spaces had been piled high with corpses, whose spirit had died, Gillian Perholt felt, but maybe felt because she could not feel the new spirit, which spoke to this family, and in them filled her with fear. Orhan, she saw, was in some way enjoying himself. He prolonged the conversation, nodding gravely, inserting mild questions – 'you have seen signs, mn?' – making no move to change his interlocutor's impression that he was a good Muslim, in a mosque.

His family came everywhere with him, said the pilgrim. They like to see new places. And she, does she speak English?

It was clear that Gillian had been taken for a quiet Muslim wife. She had been standing two paces behind Orhan as he cast about for the magic pillar. Orhan replied gravely:

'She *is* English. She is a visiting professor. An eminent visiting professor.'

Orhan, a child of Atatürk's new world, was enjoying himself. Atatürk had emancipated women. Leyla Serin and Leyla Doruk were also his children, powerful people, thinking teachers. Orhan liked drama, and he had made a nice little revelatory clash. The Pakistani gentleman was not happy. He and Gillian looked at each other, both, she thought, remembering things he had said a moment ago about London being a sewer of decay and the Commonwealth a dead body, putrefying and shrivelling away to nothing. She could not meet the Pakistani's eye; she was English and embarrassed for him. He could not meet her eye. She was a woman, and should not have been there, with a man who was not her husband, in a museum that was also a mosque. He gathered his flock – who still smiled at Gillian, fluttering their elegant fingers in farewell. 'Hrmph,' said Orhan. 'Istanbul is a meeting-place for many cultures. You didn't like the pillar, Gillian? Your face was very funny, very ladylike.'

'I don't like Haghia Sophia,' said Gillian. 'I expected to. I like the idea of Sophia, of Wisdom, I like it that she is wise and female, I expected to feel – something – in her church. And there is a wet hole for fertility wishes. In a pillar that might have come from the Temple of Artemis.'

'Not that pillar, I think,' said Orhan.

'If I was a postmodernist punster,' said Gillian, 'I would make something of Haghia Sophia. She has got old, she has turned into a Hag. But I can't, because I respect etymologies, it means holy. Hag is my word, a northern word, nothing to do with here.'

'You have said it now,' said Orhan. 'Even if you repudiate it. Lots of American students here do think Hag is Hag. They get excited about Crones.'

'I don't,' said Gillian.

'No,' said Orhan, not revealing what he himself thought about hags and crones. 'We shall go to the Bazaar. Shopping is good for the souls of western women. And eastern. And men like it too.'

It was true that the Grand Bazaar was livelier and brighter than the vast cavern of Haghia Sophia.

Here was a warren of arcades, of Aladdin's caves full of lamps and magical carpets, of silver and brass and gold and pottery and tiles. Here and there behind a shop-front, seated in an armchair at a bench surrounded by dangling lamps and water-shakers from the baths, or sitting cross-legged on a bale of carpets amongst a tent of carpets, Orhan had ex-students who brought cups of Turkish coffee, tulip-shaped glasses of rose tea to Gillian, and displayed their wares. The carpet-seller had written a Ph.D. on *Tristram Shandy*, and now travelled into Iraq, Iran, Afghanistan, bringing back carpets on journeys made by camel, by jeep, into the mountains. He showed Gillian pallid kilims in that year's timid Habitat colours, pale 1930s eau-de-nil and bois-de-rose with a sad null grey. No, said Gillian, no, she wanted richness, the dark bright blues, the crimsons and scarlets, the golds and rusts of the old carpets with their creamy blossoms, their trees full of strange birds and flowers. The West is fickle, said Bulent the carpet-seller, they say they want these insipid colours this year, and the women in India and Iran buy the wool and the silk, and the next year, when the carpets are made, they want something else, black and purple and orange, and the women are ruined, their profit is lost, heaps of carpets lie round and rot. I think you will like this carpet, said Bulent, pouring coffee; it is a wedding carpet, a dowry carpet, to hang on the wall of a nomad's tent. Here is the tree of life, crimson and black on midnight blue. This you like. Oh yes, said Gillian, seeing the dark woven tree against the yellows and whites of her Primrose Hill room, now hers alone. The woman, whoever she was, had made it strong and complex, flaunting and subtle. I can't haggle, said Gillian to Orhan, I'm English. You would be surprised, said Orhan, at some English people's skill in that art. But Bulent is my student, and he will give you a fair price, for love of *Tristram Shandy*. And suddenly Gillian felt well again, full of life and singing with joy, away from the puddle in the pillar and the brooding Hag, hidden away in an Aladdin's cave made of magic carpets with small delightful human artefacts, an unknown woman's wedding carpet, sentimental Sterne's monumental fantasia on life before birth, black-brown coffee poured from a bright copper pan, tasting rich and almost, but not quite, unbearably strong and sweet.

Another of Orhan's students had a little shop in the central square of the market-maze, Iç Bedesten, a shop whose narrow walls were entirely hung with pots, pans, lamps, bottles, leather objects, old tools whose purpose was unguessable, chased daggers and hunting knives, shadow-puppets made of camel skin, perfume flasks, curling tongs.

'I will give you a present,' said Orhan. 'A present to say good-bye.'

(He was leaving the next day for Texas where a colloquium of narratologists was studying family sagas in Dallas. Gillian had a talk to give at the British Council and three more days in Istanbul.)

'I will give you the shadow puppets, Karagöz and Hacivat, and here is the magic bird, the Simurgh, and here is a woman involved with a dragon, I think she may be a djinee, with a little winged demon on her shoulders, you might like her.'

The small figures were wrapped carefully in scarlet tissue. Whilst this was happening Gillian poked about on a bench and found a bottle, a very dusty bottle amongst an apparently unsorted pile of new/old things. It was a flask with a high neck, that fitted comfortably into the palms of her hands, and had a glass stopper like a miniature dome. The whole was dark, with a regular whirling pattern of white stripes moving round it. Gillian collected glass paperweights: she liked glass in general, for its paradoxical nature, translucent as water, heavy as stone, invisible as air, solid as earth. Blown with human breath in a furnace of fire. As a child she had loved to read of glass balls containing castles and snowstorms, though in reality she had always found these disappointing and had transferred her magical attachment to the weights in which coloured forms and carpets of geometric flowers shone perpetually and could be made to expand and contract as the sphere of glass turned in her fingers in the light. She liked to take a weight back from every journey, if one could be found, and had already bought a Turkish weight, a cone of glass like a witch's hat, rough to touch, greenish-transparent like ice, with the concentric circles, blue, yellow, white, blue, of the eye which repels the evil eye, at the base.

'What is this?' she asked Orhan's student, Feyyaz.

He took the flask from her, and rubbed at the dust with a finger.

'I'm not an expert in glass,' he said. 'It could be çesm-i bülbül, nightingale's eye. Or it could be fairly recent Venetian glass. Çesm-i bülbül means nightingale's eye. There was a famous Turkish glass workshop at Incirköy – round about 1845 I think – made this famous Turkish glass, with this spiral pattern of opaque blue and white stripes, or red sometimes, I think. I don't know why it is called eye of the nightingale. Perhaps nightingales have eyes that are transparent and opaque. In this country we were obsessed with nightingales. Our poetry is full of nightingales.'

'Before pollution,' said Orhan, 'before television, everyone came out and walked along the Bosphorus and in all the gardens, to hear the first nightingales of the year. It was very beautiful. Like the Japanese and the cherry blossom. A whole people, walking quietly in the spring weather, listening.'

Feyyaz recited a verse in Turkish and Orhan translated.

In the woods full of evening the nightingales are silent
The river absorbs the sky and its fountains
Birds return to the indigo shores from the shadows
A scarlet bead of sunshine in their beaks.

Gillian said, 'I must have this. Because the word and the thing don't quite match, and I love both of them. But if it is çesm-i bülbül it will be valuable . . .'

'It probably isn't,' said Feyyaz. 'It's probably recent Venetian. Our glassmakers went to Venice in the eighteenth century to learn, and the Venetians helped us to develop the techniques of the nineteenth century. I will sell it to you as if it were Venetian, because you like it, and you may imagine it is çesm-i bülbül and perhaps it will be, is, that is.'

'Feyyaz wrote his doctoral thesis on Yeats and Byzantium,' said Orhan.

Gillian gave the stopper an experimental twist, but it would not come away, and she was afraid of breaking it. So the nightingale's-eye bottle too was wrapped in scarlet tissue, and more rose tea was sipped, and Gillian returned to her hotel. That evening there was a farewell dinner in Orhan's house, with music, and rakı, and generous beautiful food. And the next day, Gillian was alone in her hotel room.

Time passes differently in the solitude of hotel rooms. The mind expands, but lazily, and the body contracts in its bright box of space. Because one may think of anything at all, one thinks for a long time of nothing. Gillian in hotel rooms was always initially tempted by channel-surfing on the television; she lay amongst crimson and creamy roses on her great bed and pointed the black lozenge with its bright buttons imperiously at the screen. Transparent life flickered and danced across it: Gillian could make it boom with sound, the rush of traffic and violins, voices prophesying war and voices dripping with the promise of delectable yogurt/ Orangina/tutti-frutti/Mars Bars frozen stiff. Or she could leave it, which she preferred, a capering shadow-theatre. Ronald Reagan, smiling and mouthing, glassy in the glass box between the glassy wings of his speech, or an aeroplane falling in flames on a mountain, fact or stunt? a priest driving a racing-car round a corniche, narrative or advertisement? Turks discussing the fullness and fatness of tomatoes in a field, more new cars, in cornfields, up mountains, falling from skyscrapers, a houri applying a tongue tip to raspberry fudge and sighing, an enormous tsetse fly expending enormous energy in puncturing a whole screenful of cowflesh, jeeps full of dirty soldiers in helmets brandishing machine-guns, trundling through dusty streets, fact or drama, which? tennis.

Tennis in French, from courts like red deserts, tennis from Monte Carlo where it was high noon, under the sun past which Istanbul had begun to roll two hours ago, tennis male and it appeared, live, on a channel where nothing ever happened but the human body (and mind, indeed, also) stretched, extended, driven, triumphant, defeated, in one endless, beautifully designed narrative. Dr Perholt was accustomed to say, in her introductory talks on narratology, that whoever designed the rules and the scoring-system of tennis was a narrative genius of the first order, comparable to those ancient storytellers who arranged animal-helpers in threes and thought up punishments for disregarded prohibitions. For the more even the combat, said Dr Perholt, the more difficult the scoring makes it for one combatant to succeed. At deuce, at six-all, the stakes are raised, not one but two points are needed to assure victory, not one but two games, thus ensuring the maximum tension and the maximum pleasure to the watchers. Tennis in the glass box she loved as she had loved bedtime stories as a child. She loved the skill of the cameramen – the quick shot of a sweating face in a rictus of strain, the balletic shot of the impossibly precise turning feet, the slow lazy repeat of the lung-bursting leap, taken at the speed with which a leaf falls slowly through the air, slowly, slowly, resting on air, as the camera can make these heavy muscled men hang at rest in their billowing shirts. She had only come to love tennis so much when she was beyond being expected to take part in it; when her proper function was only as audience. Now she delighted in its geometry, the white lines of increasing difficulty, of hope and despair, the acid gold sphere of the ball, the red dust flying, the woven chequered barrier of the net. She had her narrative snobbisms. A live match was always more enticing than a recorded one, even if it was impossible for her to find out first the score of the latter, for someone, somewhere, *knew* who had won, the tense was past, and thus the wonderful open-endedness of a story which is most beautifully designed towards satisfactory closure but is still undecided, would be lost, would be a cheat. For darkness might descend on a live match, or the earth open. A live match was live, was a story in progress towards an end which had not yet come but which must, *almost certainly* come. And in the fact of the *almost* was the delight.

A live match (Becker-Leconte) was promised within an hour. She had time for a shower, she judged, a good hot shower, and then she could sit and dry slowly and watch the two men run. So she turned on the shower, which was large and brassy, behind a glass screen at one end of the bath, an enclosing screen of pleasing engraved climbing roses with little birds sitting amongst their thorny stems. It had a pleasant brass frame, the glass box. The water was a little cloudy, and a little brassy itself in colour, but it was hot, and Gillian disported herself in its jets, soaped her breasts, shampooed her hair, looked ruefully down at what it was better not to look at, the rolls of her midriff, the sagging muscles of her stomach. She remembered, as she reached for her towel, how perhaps ten years ago she had looked complacently at her skin on her throat, at her solid enough breasts and had thought herself well-preserved, unexceptionable. She had tried to imagine how this nice, taut, flexible skin would crimp and wrinkle and fall and had not been able to. It was her skin, it was herself, and there was no visible reason why it should not persist. She had known intellectually that it must, it must give way, but its liveliness then had given her the lie. And now it was all going, the eyelids had soft little folds, the edges of the lips were fuzzed, if she put on lipstick it ran in little threads into the surrounding skin.

She advanced naked towards the bathroom mirror in room 49 in the Peri Palas Hotel. The mirror was covered with shifting veils of steam, amongst which, vaguely, Gillian saw her death advancing towards her, its hair streaming dark and liquid, its eyeholes dark smudges, its mouth open in its liquescent face in fear of their convergence. She dropped her head sadly, turned aside from the encounter, and took out the hanging towelling robe from its transparent sheath of plastic. There were white towelling slippers in the cupboard with Peri Palas written on them in gold letters. She made herself a loose turban of a towel and thus solidly enveloped she remembered the çesm-i bül-bül bottle and decided to run it under the tap, to bring the glass to life. She took it out of its wrappings – it was really *very* dusty, almost clay-encrusted – and carried it into the bathroom where she turned on the mixer-tap in the basin, made the water warm, blood-heat, and held the bottle under the jet, turning it round and round. The glass became blue, threaded with opaque white canes, cobalt-blue, darkly bright, gleaming and wonderful. She turned it and turned it, rubbing the tenacious dust-spots with thumbs and fingers, and suddenly it gave a kind of warm leap in her hand, like a frog, like a still-beating heart in the hands of a surgeon. She gripped and clasped and steadied, and her own heart took a fierce, fast beat of apprehension, imagining blue glass splinters everywhere. But all that happened was that the stopper, with a faint glassy grinding, suddenly flew out of the neck of the flask and fell, tinkling but unbroken, into the basin. And out of the bottle in her hands came a swarming, an exhalation, a fast-moving dark stain which made a high-pitched buzzing sound and smelled of woodsmoke, of cinnamon, of sulphur, of something that might have been incense, of something that was not leather, but was? The dark cloud gathered and turned and flew in a great paisley or comma out of the bathroom. I am seeing things, thought Dr Perholt, following, and found she could not follow, for the bathrorom door was blocked by what she slowly made out to be an enormous foot, a foot with five toes as high as she was, surmounted by yellow horny toenails, a foot encased in skin that was olive-coloured, laced with gold, like snakeskin, not scaly but somehow mailed. It was between transparent and solid. Gillian put out a hand. It was palpable, and very hot to the touch, not hot as a coal but considerably hotter than the water in which she had been washing the bottle. It was dry and slightly electric. A vein beat inside the ankle, a green-gold tube encasing an almost emerald liquid.

Gillian stood and considered the foot. Anything with a foot that size, if at all proportionate, could not be contained in one hotel room. Where was the rest? As she thought this, she heard sounds, which seemed to be speech of some kind, deep, harsh, but musical, expletives perhaps, in a language she couldn't identify. She put the stopper back in the bottle, clutching it firmly, and waited.

The foot began to change shape. At first it swelled and then it diminished a little, so that Gillian could have squeezed round it, but thought it more prudent not to try. It was now the size of a large armchair, and was drawn back, still diminishing, so that Gillian felt able to follow. The strange voice was still muttering, in its incomprehensible speech. Gillian came out and saw the djinn, who now took up half her large room, curled round on himself like a snake, with his huge head and shoulders pushing against the ceiling, his arms stretched round inside two walls, and his feet and body wound over her bed and trailing into the room. He seemed to be wearing a green silk tunic, not too clean, and not long enough, for she could see the complex heap of his private parts in the very centre of her rosy bed. Behind him was a great expanse of shimmering many-coloured feathers, peacock feathers, parrot feathers, feathers from birds of Paradise, which appeared to be part of a cloak that appeared to be part of him, but was not wings that sprouted in any conventional way from shoulder-blade or spine. Gillian identified the last ingredient of his smell, as he moved his cramped members to look down on her. It was a male smell, a strong horripilant male smell.

His face was huge, oval, and completely hairless. He had huge bruised-green oval eyelids over eyes sea-green flecked with malachite. He had high cheekbones and an imperious hooked nose, and his mouth was wide and sculpted like Egyptian pharaohs'.

In one of his huge hands was the television, on whose pearly screen, on the red dust, Boris Becker and Henri Leconte rushed forward, jumped back, danced, plunged. The smack of the tennis ball could be heard, and the djinn had turned one of his large, elegantly carved ears, to listen.

He spoke to Gillian. She said,

'I don't suppose you speak English.'

He repeated his original remark. Gillian said,

'Français? Deutsch? Español? Português?' She hesitated. She could not remember the Latin for Latin, and was not at all sure she could converse in that language. 'Latin,' she said finally.

Je sçais le Français,' said the djinn. *'Italiano anche. Era in Venezia.*'

Je préfère le français,' said Gillian. 'I am more fluent in that language.'

'Good,' said the djinn in French. He said, 'I can learn quickly, what is your language?'

'Anglais.'

'Smaller would be better,' he said, changing tack. 'It was agreeable to expand. I have been inside that bottle since 1850 by your reckoning.'

'You look cramped,' said Gillian, reaching for the French words, 'in here.'

The djinn considered the tennis players.

'Everything is relative. These people are extremely small. I shall diminish somewhat.'

He did so, not all at once, so that for a moment the now only slightly larger-than-life being was almost hidden behind the mound of his private parts, which he then shrank and tucked away. It was almost a form of boasting. He was now curled on Gillian's bed, only one and a half times as large as she was.

'I am beholden to you,' said the djinn, 'for this release. I am empowered, indeed required, to grant you three wishes on that account. If there is anything you desire.'

'Are there limits,' asked the narratologist, 'to what I may wish for?'

'An unusual question,' said the djinn. He was still somewhat distracted by the insect-like drama of Boris Becker and Henri Leconte. 'In fact different djinns have different powers. Some can only grant small things – '

'Like sausages – '

'A believer – a believing djinn – would find it repugnant to grant anyone of your religion pork sausages. But they are possible. There are laws of the praeternatural within which we work, all of us, which cannot be broken. You may not, for instance, wish to have all your wishes granted in perpetuity. Three is three, a number of power. You may not wish for eternal life, for it is your nature to be mortal, as it is mine to be immortal. I cannot by magic hold together your atomies, which will dissolve – '

He said,

'It is good to speak again, even in this unaccustomed tongue. Can you tell me what these small men are made of, and what they are at? It resembles royal tennis as it was played in the days of Suleiman the Magnificent – '

'It is called "lawn tennis" in my language. *Tennis sur gazon*. As you can see, this is being played on clay. I like to watch it. The men,' she found herself saying, 'are very beautiful.'

'Indeed,' agreed the djinn. 'How have you enclosed them? The atmosphere here is full of presences I do not understand – it is all bustling and crowded with – I cannot find a word in my language or your own, that is, your second tongue, – electrical emanations of living beings, and not only living beings but fruits and flowers and distant places – and some high mathematical game with travelling figures I can barely seize, like motes in the invisible air – something terrible has been done to my space – to exterior space since my incarcer-ation – I have trouble in holding this exterior body together, for all the currents of power are so picked at and intruded upon . . . Are these men magicians, or are you a witch, that you have them in a box?'

'No, it is science. It is natural science. It is televi-sion. It is done with light waves and sound waves and cathode rays – I don't know *how* it is done, I am only a literary scholar, we don't know much, I'm afraid – we use it for information and amusement. Most people in the world now see these boxes, I suppose.'

'*Six-all, première manche,*' said the television. *Jeu décisif. Service Becker.*'

The djinn frowned.

'I am a djinn of some power,' he said. I begin to find out how these emanations travel. Would you like a homunculus of your own?'

'I have three wishes,' said Dr Perholt cautiously. 'I do not want to expend one of them on the posses-sion of a tennis-player.'

'*Entendu,*' said the djinn. 'You are an intelligent and cautious woman. You may wish when you will and the praeternatural laws require me to remain at your service until all three wishes have been made. Lesser djinns would tempt you into making your wishes rapidly and foolishly, for their own ends, but I am God-fearing and honourable (despite which I have spent much of my long life shut up in bottles), and I will not do that. All the same, I shall attempt to catch one of these travelling butterflies. They are spread along the waves of the atmosphere – not as we are when we travel – *in* the waves – I should be able to *concentrate* one – to move the matter as well as the emanation – the pleasure is to use the laws of its appearance here and intensify – I could easily *wish* him here – but I will, I will have him along his own trajectory – so – and so – '

A small Boris Becker, sandy-browed, every gold hair on his golden body gleaming sweat, was standing on the chest of drawers, perhaps twice the size of his television image, which was frozen in mid-stroke on the screen. He blinked his sandy lashes over his blue eyes and looked around, obviously unable to see more than a blur around him.

'*Scheisse,*' said the tiny Becker. '*Scheisse und scheisse. Was ist mit mir?*'

'I could manifest us to him,' said the djinn. 'He would be afeard.'

'Put him back. He will lose the set.'

'I could expand him. Life-size. We could speak to him.'

'Put him back. It isn't *fair.*'

'You don't want him?'

'*Scheisse. Warum kann ich nicht . . .*'

'No. I don't.'

The Becker on the screen was frozen into an attitude, his racket raised, his head back, one foot lifting. Henri Leconte advanced towards the net. The commentator announced that Becker had had a seizure, which delighted the djinn, who had indeed seized him. '*Scheisse,*' said the forlorn small Becker in the bedroom. 'Return him,' said Dr Perholt imperiously, adding quickly, 'That is not one of my three wishes, you must do what seems to you best, but you must understand that you are disappointing millions of people, all round the world, interrupting this story – I'm sorry, *déformation professionelle,* I should say, this game – '

'Why are your homunculi not three-dimensional?' asked the djinn.

'I don't know. We can't do that. We may learn. You seem to understand it better than I do, however long you have been in that bottle. Please put him back.'

'To please you,' said the djinn with grave gallantry. He picked up the mannikin-Becker, twisted him rapidly like a top, murmured something, and the Becker on the screen collapsed on the court in a heap.

'You have hurt him,' said Gillian accusingly.

'It is to be hoped not,' said the djinn with an uncertain note. Becker in Monte Carlo got up unsteadily and was escorted off the court, his hands to his head.

'They will not be able to continue,' said Gillian crossly, and then put her hand to her mouth in amazement, that a woman with a live djinn on her bed should still be interested in the outcome of a tennis match, only part of which she had seen.

'You could wish him well,' said the djinn, 'but he will probably be well anyway. More than probably, almost certainly. You must wish for your heart's desire.'

'I wish,' said Gillian, 'for my body to be as it was when I last really *liked* it, if you can do that.'

The great green eyes settled on her stout figure in its white robe and turban.

'I can do that,' he said. 'I can do that. If you are quite sure that that is what you most desire. I can make your cells as they were, but I cannot delay your Fate.'

'It is courteous of you to tell me that. And yes, it is what I desire. It is what I have desired hopelessly every day these last ten years, whatever else I may have desired.'

'And yet,' said the djinn, 'you are well enough as you are, in my opinion. Amplitude, madame, is desirable.'

'Not in my culture. And moreover, there is the question of temporal decay.'

'That I suppose, but do not wholly understand sympathetically. We are made of fire, and do not decay. You are made of dust, and return to it.'

He raised his hand and pointed at her, one finger lazily extended, a little like Michelangelo's Adam.

She felt a fierce contraction in the walls of her belly, in her loose womb.

'I am glad to see you prefer ripe women to green girls,' said the djinn. 'I too am of that opinion. But your ideal is a little meagre. Would you not care to be rounder?'

'Excuse me,' said Gillian, suddenly modest, and retreated into the bathroom, where she opened her robe and saw in the demisted mirror a solid and unexceptionable thirty-five-year-old woman, whose breasts were full but not softened, whose stomach was taut, whose thighs were smooth, whose nipples were round and rosy. Indeed the whole of this serviceable and agreeable body was flushed deep rose, as though she had been through a fire, or a steam bath. Her appendix scar was still there, and the mark on her knee where she had fallen on a broken bottle hiding under the stairs from an air raid in 1944. She studied her face in the mirror; it was not beautiful but it was healthy and lively and unexceptionable; her neck was a clean column and her teeth, she was happy to see and feel, more numerous, more securely planted. She undid the coiled towel and her hair sprang out, damp, floppy, long and unfaded. I can go in the streets, she said to herself, and still be recognisably who I am, in my free and happy life; only I shall *feel* better, I shall like myself more. That was an *intelligent* wish, I shall not regret it. She brushed out her hair, and went back to the djinn, who was lolling on the bed-spread, watching Boris Becker, who had lost the first set, and was ranging the court like a tiger in the beginning of the second. The djinn had also helped himelf to the glossy shopping magazines which lay in the drawer of the bedside table, and to the Gideon Bible which, with the Koran, was also there. From these he appeared to have absorbed the English language by some kind of cerebral osmosis.

'Hmn,' he said in that language, 'Who is she that looketh forth as the morning, fair as the moon, clear as the sun, and terrible as an army with banners? This is your language, I can learn its rules quickly, I find. Are you pleased, madame, with the outcome of your wish? We have a little sister and she hath no breasts: what shall we do for our sister in the day when she shall be spoken for? I see from these images that in this time you prefer your ladies

without breasts, like boys. A curious form of ascet-
icism, if that is what is, or perversity possibly, it
may be. I am not a djinn who ever needed to lurk in
bathhouses to catch young boys from behind. I
have consorted with ladies of all kinds, with the
Queen of Sheba herself, with the Shulamite whose
breasts were like clusters of grapes and ripe pomegranates, whose neck was a tower of ivory and the
smell of whose nose was like apples. A boy is a boy
and a woman is a woman, my lady. But these
images have lovely eyes, they are skilful with the
kohl.'

'If you consorted with the Queen of Sheba,' said
the scholar, 'how did you come to be shut in what I
believe is at the earliest a *nineteenth-century* bottle,
çesm-i bülbül, if not Venetian?'

'Certainly çesm-i bülbül,' said the djinn. 'Freshly
made and much prized by its owner, the beautiful
Zefir, wife of Mustafa Emin Bey, in Smyrna. I came
into that bottle through a foolish accident and a
too-great fondness for the conversation of women.
That was my third incarceration: I shall be more
careful in the future. I am happy to tell you my

history, whilst you decide upon your two remain-
ing wishes, but I am also curious to know your own
– are you wife, or widow, and how do you come to
be inhabiting this splendid apartment with flowing
waters in the Peri Palas as your shining books tell
me this place is called? What I know of England is
little and unfriendly. I know the tale of the pale
slaves from the island in the north of whom a
Roman bishop said *"Non Angli sed angeli."* And I
know about Bisnismen, from the conversation in
the caravanserai in Smyrna. You are rumoured to
be thick red people who cannot bend or smile, but I
have learned never to trust rumours and I find you
graceful.'

'My name is Gillian Perholt,' said Dr Perholt. 'I
am an independent woman, a scholar, I study tale-
telling and narratology.' (She thought he could
learn this useful word; his green eyes glittered.) 'I
am in Turkey for a conference, and return to my
island in a week's time. I do not think my history
will interest you, much.'

'On the contrary. I am temporarily in your
power, and it is always wise to understand the
history of those who hold power over you. I have

lived much of my life in harems, and in harems the
study of apparently uneventful personal histories
is a matter of extreme personal importance. The
only truly independent woman I have known was
the Queen of Sheba, my half-cousin, but I see that
things have changed since her day. What does an
independent woman wish for, Djil-yan Peri-han?'

'Not much,' said Gillian, 'that I haven't got. I
need to think. I need to be intelligent. Tell me the
story of your three incarcerations. If that would not
bore you.'

She was later to wonder how she could be so mat-
ter-of-fact about the presence of the gracefully
lounging Oriental daimon in a hotel room. At the
time, she unquestioningly accepted his reality and
his remarks as she would have done if she had met
him in a dream – that is to say, with a certain difference, a certain knowledge that the reality in which
she was was not everyday, was not the reality in
which Dr Johnson refuted Bishop Berkeley's solip-
sism with a robust kick at a trundling stone. She
was accustomed also to say in lectures, that it was
possible that the human need to tell tales about

things that were unreal originated in dreams, and that memory had certain things also in common with dreams; it re-arranged, it made clear, simple narratives, certainly it invented as well as recalling. Hobbes, she told her students, had described imagination as decayed memory. She had at no point the idea that she might 'wake up' from the presence of the djinn and find him gone as though he had never been; but she did feel she might move suddenly – or he might – into some world where they no longer shared a mutual existence. But he persisted, his finger-nails and toe-nails solid and glistening, his flesh with its slightly simmering quality, his huge considering eyes, his cloak of wings, his scent, with its perfumes and smokiness, its pheromones, if djinns have pheromones, a question she was not ready to put to him. She suggested ordering a meal from Room Service, and together they chose charred vegetable salad, smoked turkey, melons and passion fruit sorbet; the djinn made himself scarce whilst this repast was wheeled in, and added to it, upon his reappearance, a bowl of fresh figs and pomegranates and some intensely rose-perfumed loukoum. Gillian said that she need not have ordered anything if he could do that, and he said that she did not allow for the effects of curiosity on one who had been cramped in a bottle since 1850 (your reckoning, he said in French) – he desired greatly to see the people and way of life of this late time.

'Your slaves,' he said, 'are healthy and smiling. That is good.'

'There are no slaves, we no longer have slaves – at least not in the west and not in Turkey – we are all free,' said Gillian, regretting this simplification as soon as it was uttered.

'No slaves,' said the djinn thoughtfully. 'No sultans, maybe, either?'

'No sultans. A republic. Here. In my country we have a Queen. She has no power. She is – a representative figure.'

'The Queen of Sheba had power,' said the djinn, folding his brow in thought, and adding dates, sherbet, quails, *marrons glacés* and two slices of *tarte aux pommes* to the feast spread before them. 'She would say to me, as her spies brought her news of his triumphal progress across the desert, the great Suleiman, blessed be his memory, she would say,

"How can I, a great Queen, submit to the prison house of marriage, to the invisible chains which bind me to the bed of a man?" I advised her against it. I told her her wisdom was hers and she was free as an eagle floating on the waves of the air and seeing the cities and palaces and mountains below her with an even eye. I told her her body was rich and lovely but her mind was richer and lovelier and more durable – for although she was partly of our kind, she was a mortal being, like you – djinns and mortals cannot produce an immortal scion, you know, as donkeys and horses can only produce a seedless mule. And she said she knew I was in the right: she sat amongst the cushions in her inner room, where no one came, and twisted her dark hair in her hand, and knit her brow in thought, and I looked at the great globes of her breasts and the narrowness of her waist and her huge soft fundament like two great heaps of silky sand, and was sick with desire for her, though I said nothing of that, for she liked to play with me a little, she had known me since she was born, I had come invisibly in and out of her sleeping-chamber and kissed her soft mouth and stroked her back as she grew, and I knew as well as any of her female slaves the little touches that made her shiver with bliss, but all was in play only, and she liked to consult me on serious matters, on the intentions of the kings of Persia and Bessarabia, on the structure of a ghazal, on medicines for choler and despair, on the disposition of the stars. And she said she knew I was right, and that her freedom was her true good, not to be surrendered, and that only I – an immortal djinn – and a few women, advised her so, but that most of her court, men and women, and her human family were in favour of marriage with this Suleiman (blessed be his memory), who advanced across the desert day by day, growing in her mind as I could grow and shrink before her eyes. And when he came, I saw that I was lost, for she desired him. It is true to say that he was desirable, his loins and his buttocks in his silk trousers were of a perfect beauty, and his fingers were long and wonderfuly quick – he could play on a woman as well as he could play on a lute or a flute – but at first she did not know that she desired him, and I, like a fool, went on telling her to think of her proud autonomy, of her power to go in and out as she pleased.

And she agreed with all I said, she nodded gravely
and once dropped a hot tear, which I licked up –
never have I desired any creature so, woman or
djinn or peri or boy like a fresh-peeled chestnut.
And then she began to set him tasks which seemed
impossible – to find a particular thread of red silk in
the whole palace, to guess the secret Name of the
djinn her mother, to tell her what women most
desire – and I knew even more surely that I was
lost, for he could speak to the beasts of the earth
and the birds of the air, and djinns from the kingdom of fire, and he found ants to discover the
thread, and an Ifrit from the kingdom of fire to tell
him the Name, and he looked into her eyes and told
her what women most desire, and she lowered her
eyes and said he was right, and granted him what *he*
desired, which was to wed her and take her to his
bed, with her lovely curtain of flesh still unparted
and her breath coming in little pants of desire that I
had never heard, never, and never should again.
And when I saw him tear her maidenhead and the
ribbon of red blood flow on to the silk sheets, I gave
a kind of groan, and he became aware of my presence. He was a great magician, blessed be his

name, and could see me well enough, though I was invisible. And he lay there, bathed in her sweat and his, and took account of certain little love-bites – most artistically placed, and unfortunately not invisible – in the soft hollows of her collar-bone, and – elsewhere, you may imagine. And he could see the virgin blood well enough, or I imagine my fate might have been worse, but he imprisoned me with a word of power in a great metal flask there was in the room, and sealed me in with his own seal, and she said nothing, she made no plea for me – though I am a believer, and not a follower of Iblis – only lay back and sighed, and I saw her tongue caress her pearly teeth, and her soft hand reach out to touch those parts of him which had given her such pleasure, and I was nothing to her, a breath in a bottle. And so I was cast into the Red Sea, with many others of my kind, and languished there for two and a half thousand years until a fisherman drew me up in his net and sold the bottle to a travelling pedlar, who took me to the bazaar in Istanbul where I was bought by a handmaid of Princess Mihrimah, daughter of Suleiman the Magnificent, and taken to the Abode of Bliss, the Eski Saray, the harem in the palace.'

'Tell me,' said Gillian Perholt, interrupting his story, 'What do women most desire?'

'Do you not know?' said the djinn. 'If you do not know already, I cannot tell you.'

'Maybe they do not all desire the same thing.'

'Maybe you do not. Your own desires, Djil-yan Peri-han, are not clear to me. I cannot read your thoughts, and that intrigues me. Will you not tell me your life?'

'It is of no interest. Tell me what happened when you were bought by Princess Mihrimah.'

'This lady was the daughter of the Sultan, Suleiman the Magnificent and his concubine Roxelana, la Rossa, the woman out of Galicia, daughter of a Ukrainian priest and known in Turkish as Hurrem, the laughing one. She was terrible as an army with the banners, Roxelana. She defeated the Sultan's early love, Gülbahar, the Rose of Spring, whom he adored, and when she bore him a son, she laughed him fiercely into marrying her, which no concubine, no Christian, had ever achieved. And when the kitchens burned – in your year 1540 it must be – she marched her household into the Seraglio – a hundred ladies-in-waiting and the eunuchs, all quaking in their shoes for fear of being disembowelled on the spot – but they were more afraid of her laughter – and so she settled in the palace itself. And Mihrimah's husband, Rüstem Pasha, was the grand vizir after Ibrahim was strangled. I remember Suleiman the Magnificent – his face was round with blue eyes, the nose of a ram, the body of a lion, a full beard, a long neck – he was a big man, a king of men, a man without fear or compromise, a glorious man. . . . Those who came after were fools and boys. That was her fault, Roxelana's fault. She intrigued against his son Mustafa, Gülbahar's son, who was like his father and would have been a wise ruler – she persuaded Suleiman he was treacherous, and so when he came boldly into his father's presence they were waiting for him, the mutes with the silk strangling cords, and he tried to cry to the janissaries who loved him, but the stranglers beat him down and stopped his breath. I saw it all, for I had been sent to see it by my new young mistress, a slave girl who belonged to Mihrimah

and opened my bottle, believing it contained perfume for her mistress's bath. She was a Christian
and a Circassian, Gülten, pale for my tastes, and
tremulous and given to weeping and wringing her
hands. And when I appeared to her in that secret
bathroom she could only faint and I had great
trouble in rousing her and explaining to her that
she had three wishes, because she had released me,
and that I meant her no harm and could do her no
harm, for I was the slave of the bottle until the
wishes were performed. And the poor silly thing
was distractedly in love with Prince Mustafa and
wished immediately that she could find favour in
his eyes. Which came about – he sent for her – I
spoke to him – I escorted her to his bedchamber, I
told her how to please him – he was very much like
his father and loved poems, and singing, and good
manners. And then the silly girl wished she could
become pregnant – '

'That was only natural.'

'Natural but very stupid. Better to use the wish
against pregnancy, my lady, and also foolish to
waste the wish in such a hurry, for they were both
young and lusty and hot-blooded, and what did

215

happen would have happened without my inter-
ference, and I could have helped her in more
important ways. For of course when Roxelana
heard that Gülten was to bear Mustafa's child, she
ordered her eunuchs to sew her up in a sack and
throw her from the Seraglio Point into the Bosphorus. And I thought to myself, having flown back
from Mustafa's execution, that at any moment she
would bethink herself of me, and wish – I don't
know exactly what – but wish to be far away – or
out of the sack – or back in Circassia – I waited for
her to formulate the wish, because once she had
made it we would both be free, I to fly where I
pleased and she to live, and bear her child. But her
limbs were frozen cold, and her lips were blue as
lapis with terror, and her great blue eyes were
starting out of her head – and the gardeners – the
executioners were also the gardeners, you know –
bundled her into the sack like a dead rosebush –
and carried her away to the cliff over the Bosphorus. And I thought of rescuing her at every moment
– but I calculated that she *must*, even involuntarily,
wish for her life, and that if I delayed, and went invisibly through the garden in the evening – the

roses were in full bloom, the perfume was intense to swooning – and over she went, and drowned, before I could quite make up my mind to the fact that she was in no state to make any wish.

So there was I, said the djinn, half-emancipated, you could say, but still tied to the bottle by the third unperformed task. I found I was free to wander during the day within a certain range of the enchanted flask, but I was compelled to return at night and shrink myself to its compass and sleep there. I was a prisoner of the harem, and likely to remain so, for my bottle was securely hidden under a tile in the floor of a bathroom, a secretly loosened tile, known only to the drowned Circassian. For women closed into those places find many secret places to hide things, for they like to have one or two possessions of their own – or a place to hide letters – that no one else, they fondly think, knows of. And I found I was unable to attract anyone's attention to the tile and the bottle; these things were out of my power.

And so I haunted the Topkapı Sarayı for just under a hundred years, attached by a silken cord you might say poetically, to the flask hidden in the bathroom floor. I saw Roxelana persuade Suleiman the Magnificent to write to the Shah Tahmasp of Persia, with whom their youngest son, Bayezid, had taken refuge, and command the Shah to execute the young Prince – which he would not do for hospitality's sake, but allowed it to be done by Turkish mutes, as was customary, and Bayezid was put to death, with his four sons and a fifth, three years of age, hidden in Bursa. He would have made an excellent ruler, too, I think – and so it was generally thought.'

'*Why?*' asked Gillian Perholt.

'It was customary, my lady, and Roxelana wished to assure a safe succession for her eldest son Selim, Selim the Sot, Selim the drunkard, Selim the poet, who died in a bathhouse after too many flasks of wine. Roxelana was long dead, buried beside the Süleymaniye, and Mihrimah her daughter built a new mosque to commemorate Suleiman, with the help of the great arthitect, Sinan, who made the Süleymaniye in holy rivalry with Haghia Sophia. And I watched sultans come and go – Murad III who was ruled by women, and strangled five of his brothers, Mehmed III who strangled nineteen of his, and then gave them sumptuous burials – he died when a dervish predicted he would live another fifty-five days – on the fifty-fifth, in fear and trembling. I watched Mustafa, the holy madman, who was brought from the cages of the princes, deposed, brought back after the slaughter of the boy Osman, and deposed by Murad IV who was the most cruel. Can you imagine a man, my lady, who could see a circle of lovely girls dancing in a meadow, and order them all to be drowned because they sang too loudly? No one spoke in those days, in the palace, for fear of attracting his attention. He could have a man killed because his teeth chattered involuntarily for fear of being put to death. And when he was dying he ordered the death of his only surviving brother, Ibrahim. But his mother, Kösem, the Greek, the Valide Sultan, lied to him and said it was done, when it was not. I saw him smile and try to get up to see the corpse, and fall back in his death-throes.

As for Ibrahim. He was a fool, a cruel fool, who loved things of the harem where he had grown up. He listened to an old storyteller in the harem – a woman from north of the Ukraine, who told him of

northern kings who made love to their concubines
in rooms entirely lined with sables, and with sables
on their couches and sables on their bodies. So he
made himself a great robe, sable without, sable
within, with great jewels for buttons, which he
wore whilst he satisfied his lust – the smell was not
good, after a time. And he believed that the pleasures of the flesh would be more intense the larger
the expanse of flesh with which he coped, so he
sent out janissaries over all his lands to seek out the
fleshiest, the hugest women, and bring them to his
couch, where he scrambled all over them dragging
the edges of his dark furs like a beast. And that is
how I came to return to my bottle, for the fattest of
all, the most voluptuous, the most like a sweet-
breathed cow, whose anklets were twice your present waist, madame – she was an Armenian
Christian, she was docile and short of breath – it
was she who was so heavy that she dislodged the
tile under which my bottle lay concealed – and so I
stood before her in the bathroom and she wheezed
with anxiety. I told her that the Valide Sultan
planned to have her strangled that night at the ban-
quet she was dressing for, and I thought she would

utter a wish – wish herself a thousand miles away, or wish that someone would strangle the Valide Sultan – or even wish a small wish, such as 'I wish I knew what to do', and I would have told her what to do, and rushed on wide wings to the ends of the earth afterwards.

But this globular lady was self-satisfied and slow-witted, and all she could think of to say was 'I wish you were sealed up in your bottle again, infidel Ifrit, for I want nothing to do with dirty djinns. You smell bad,' she added, as I coiled myself back into atomies of smoke and sighed myself into the flask and replaced the stopper. And she carried my flask through the rose-garden where my white Circassian had been carried, and threw me over the Seraglio Point into the Bosphorus. She undertook this herself; I could feel the voluptuous rippling and juddering of her flesh as she progressed along the paths. I was about to say she had not taken so much exercise in years, but that would be unjust – she had to use her musculature very vigorously in certain ways to cope with the more extreme projects of Sultan Ibrahim. And Kösem did have her strangled that night, just as I had told her. It would have been more interesting to have been released by those doughty Sultanas, by Roxelana or Kösem, but my luck was femininity.

And so I tossed about in the Bosphorus for another two hundred and fifty years and was then fished up by another fisherman and sold as an antique to a merchant of Smyrna, who gave me – or my flask – as a love-token to his young wife Zefir, who had a collection of curious-shaped bottles and jars in her quarters in the harem. And Zefir saw the seal on the bottle and knew what it was, for she was a great reader of tales and histories. She told me later she spent all night in fear, wondering whether to open the flask, in case I might be angry, like the djinn who threatened to kill his rescuer because he had become enraged over the centuries, that the poor man had taken so long to come to his aid. But she was a brave creature, Zefir, and ardent for knowledge, and mortally bored, so one day, alone in her chamber she pushed away the seal. . . .'

'What was she like?' said Gillian, since the djinn appeared to have floated off into a reminiscent reverie.

His eyelids were half-closed and the edges of his huge nostrils fluttered.

'Ah,' he said, 'Zefir. She had been married at fourteen to the merchant who was older than she was, and was kind enough to her, kind enough, if you call treating someone like a toy dog or a spoiled baby or a fluffy fat bird in a cage being kind. She was good-looking enough, a sharp, dark person, with secret black-brown eyes and an angry line of a mouth that pulled in at the corners. She was wayward and angry, Zefir, and she had nothing at all to do. There was an older wife who didn't like her and didn't talk to her, and servants, who seemed to her to be mocking her. She spent her time sewing huge pictures in silk – pictures of stories – the stories from the Shahnama, of Rüstem and the Shah Kaykavus who tried to emulate the djinns and fly, and devised a method of some ingenuity – he tied four strong yet hungry eagles to a throne, and four juicy legs of mutton to the rising posts of the canopy of the throne – and then he seated himself, and the eagles strove to reach the meat, and lifted the throne – and the shah – towards the heavens. But the eagles tired, and the throne and its occupant fell to earth – she had embroidered him coming down headlong and head first, and she had sewed him a rich carpet of flowers to fall on, for she thought him aspiring, and not a fool. You should have seen the beauty of her silk legs of mutton, like the life – or rather, death. She was a great artist, Zefir, but no one saw her art. And she was angry because she knew she was capable of many things she couldn't even define to herself, so they seemed like bad dreams – that is what she told me. She told me she was eaten up with unused power and thought she might be a witch – except, she said, if she were a man, these things she thought about would be ordinarily acceptable. If she had been a man, and a westerner, she would have rivalled the great Leonardo whose flying machines were the talk of the court of Suleiman one summer –

'So I taught her mathematics, which was bliss to her, and astronomy, and many languages, she studied secretly with me, and poetry – we wrote an epic poem about the travels of the Queen of Sheba – and history, I taught her the history of Turkey and the history of the Roman Empire, and the history of the Holy Roman Empire – I bought her novels in many languages, and philosophical treatises, Kant and Descartes and Leibnitz – '

'Wait,' said Gillian. 'Was this her wish, that you should teach her these things?'

'Not exactly,' said the djinn. 'She wished to be wise and learned, and I had known the Queen of Sheba, and what it was to be a wise woman . . .'

'Why did she not wish to *get out of there?*' asked Gillian.

'I advised against it. I said the wish was bound to go wrong, unless she was better-informed about the possible places or times she might wish herself into – I said there was no hurry –'

'You enjoyed teaching her.'

'Rarely among humankind can there have been a more intelligent being,' said the djinn. 'And not only intelligent.' He brooded.

'I taught her other things also,' he said. 'Not at first. At first I flew in and out with bags of books and papers and writing things that I then hid by temporarily vanishing them into her bottle collection – so she could always call on Aristotle from the red glass perfume-bottle, or Euclid from the green tear-bottle, without needing me to re-embody them – '

'And did that count as a wish?' asked Gillian severely.

'Not really.' The djinn was evasive. 'I taught her a few magical skills – to help her – because I loved her – '

'You loved her – '

'I loved her anger. I loved my own power to change her frowns to smiles. I taught her what her husband had not taught her, to enjoy her own body, without all the gestures of submission and non-disturbance of his own activities the silly man seemed to require.'

'You were in no hurry for her to escape – to exercise her new powers somewhere else – '

'No. We were happy. I like being a teacher. It is unusual in djinns – we have a natural propensity to trick and mislead your kind. But your kind is rarely as greedy for knowledge as Zefir. I had all the time in the world – '

'*She* didn't,' said Gillian who was trying to feel her way into this story, occluded by the djinn's own feelings, it appeared. She felt a certain auto-matic resentment of this long-dead Turkish prodigy, the thought of whom produced the dreaming smile on the lips of what she had come to think of – so quickly – as *her* djinn. But she also felt troubled on Zefir's behalf, by the djinn's desire to be both liberator and imprisoner in one.

'I know,' said the djinn. 'She was mortal, I know. What year is it now?'

'It is 1991.'

'She would be one hundred and sixty-four years old, if she lived. And our child would be one hundred and forty, which is not possible for such a being.'

'A child?'

'Of fire and dust. I planned to fly with him round the earth, and show him the cities and the forests and the shores. He would have been a great genius – maybe. I don't know if he was ever born.'

'Or she.'

'Or she. Indeed.'

'What happened? Did she wish for *anything at all?* Or did you prevent her to keep her prisoner?

How did you come to be in my çesm-i bülbül bottle? I do not understand.'

'She was a very clever woman, like you, Djil-yan, and she knew it was wise to wait. And then – I think – I know – she began to wish – to desire – that I should stay with her. We had a whole world in her little room. I brought things from all over the world – silks and satins, sugar-cane and paw-paw, sheets of green ice, Donatello's Perseus, aviaries full of parrots, waterfalls, rivers. One day, un-guardedly, she wished she could fly with me when I went to the Americas, and then she could have bitten off her tongue, and almost wasted a second wish undoing the first, but I put a finger on her lip – she was so quick, she understood in a flash – and I kissed her, and we flew to Brazil, and to Paraguay, and saw the Amazon river which is as great as a sea, and the beasts in the forests there, where no man treads, and she was blissfully warm against my heart inside the feathered cloak – there are spirits with feathered cloaks out there, we found, whom we met in the air above the forest canopy – and then I brought her back to her room, and she fainted with joy and disappointment.'

He came to another halt, and Dr Perholt, savouring loukoum, had to encourage him.

'So she had two wishes. And became pregnant. Was she happy to be pregnant?'

'Naturally, in a way, she was happy, to be carrying a magic child. And naturally, in another, she was afraid: she said perhaps she should ask for a magic palace where she could bring up the child in safety in a hidden place – but that was not what she wanted – she said also she was not sure she wanted a child at all, and came near wishing him out of existence – '

'But you saved him.'

'I loved her. He was mine. He was a small seed, like a curved comma of smoke in a bottle; he grew and I watched him. She loved me, I think, she could not wish him undone.'

'Or her. Or perhaps you could see which it was?'
He considered.

'No. I did not see. I supposed, a son.'

'But you never saw him born.'

'We quarrelled. Often. I told you she was angry. By nature. She was like a squall of sudden shower, thunder and lightning. She berated me. She said I had ruined her life. Often. And then we played again. I would make myself small, and hide. One day, to amuse her, I hid in the new çesm-i bülbül bottle that her husband had given her: I flowed in gracefully and curled myself; and she began suddenly to weep and rail and said "I wish I could forget I had ever seen you." And so she did. On the instant.'

'But – ' said Dr Perholt.

'But?' said the genie.

'But why did you not just flow out of the bottle again? Solomon had not sealed that bottle – '

'I had taught her a few sealing-spells, for pleasure. For my pleasure, in being in her power, and hers, in having power. There are humans who play such games of power with manacles and ropes. Being inside a bottle has certain things – a *few* things – in common with being inside a woman – a certain pain that at times is indistinguishable from pleasure. We cannot die, but at the moment of becoming infinitesimal inside the neck of a flask, or a jar, or a bottle – we can shiver with the apprehension of extinction – as humans speak of dying when they reach the height of bliss, in love. To be nothing, in the bottle – to pour my seed into her – it was a little the same. And I taught her the words of power as a kind of wager – a form of gambling. Russian roulette,' said the djinn, appearing to pluck these unlikely words from the air.

'So I was in, and she was out, and had forgotten me,' he concluded.

'And now,' said the djinn, 'I have told you the history of my incarcerations, and you must tell me your history.'

'I am a teacher. In a university. I was married and now I am free. I travel the world in aeroplanes and talk about storytelling.'

'Tell me your story.'

A kind of panic overcame Dr Perholt. It seemed to her that she had no story, none that would interest this hot person with his searching look and his restless intelligence. She could not tell him the history of the western world since Zefir had mistakenly wished him forgotten in a bottle of çesm-i bülbül glass, and without that string of wonders, how could he understand her?

He put a great hand on her towelled shoulder. Through the towel, even, his hand was hot and dry.

'Tell me anything,' said the djinn.

She found herself telling him how she had been a girl at a boarding-school in Cumberland, a school full of girls, a school with nowhere to hide from gaggles and klatsches of girls. It may be she told him this because of her imagined vision of Zefir, in the women's quarters in Smyrna in 1850. She told him about the horror of dormitories full of other people's sleeping breath. I am a naturally *solitary* creature, the Doctor told the djinn. She had written a secret book, her first book, she told him, during this imprisonment, a book about a young man called Julian who was in hiding, disguised as a girl called Julienne, in a similar place. In hiding from an assassin or a kidnapper, she could barely remember, at this distance, she told the djinn. Her voice faded. The djinn was impatient. Was she a lover of women in those days? No, said Dr Perholt, she believed she had written the story out of an emptiness, a need to imagine a boy, a man, the Other. And how did the story progress, asked the djinn, and could you not find a real boy or man, how did you resolve it? I could not, said Dr Perholt. It seemed silly, in writing, I could see it was silly. I filled it with details, realistic details, his underwear, his problems with gymnastics, and the more realism I tried to insert into what was really a cry of desire – desire for nothing specific – the more silly my story. It should have been farce or fable, I see that now, and I was writing passion and tragedy and buttons done with verisimilitude. I burned it in the school furnace. My imagination failed. I got all enmeshed in what was realism and what was reality and what was true – my need not to be in that place – and my imagination failed. Indeed it may be because Julian/Julienne was such a ludicrous figure that I am a narratologist and not a maker of fictions. I tried to conjure him up – he had long black hair in the days when all Englishmen had short back-and-sides – but he remained resolutely absent, or almost absent. Not quite. From time to time, he had a sort of being, he was a sort of wraith. Do you understand this?'

'Not entirely,' said the djinn. 'He was an emanation, like this Becker you would not let me give you.'

'Only the emanation of an absence.' She paused. 'When I was younger there was a boy who was real.'

'Your first lover.'

'No. No. Not flesh and blood. A golden boy who walked beside me wherever I went. Who sat beside me at table, who lay beside me at night, who sang with me, who walked in my dreams. Who disappeared when I had a headache or was sick, but was always there when I couldn't move for asthma. His name was Tadzio, I don't know where I got that from, he came with it, one day, I just looked up and I saw him. He told me stories. In a language only we two spoke. One day I found a poem which said how it was, to live in his company. I did not know anyone else knew, until I read that poem.'

'I know those beings – ' said the djinn. 'Zefir had known one. She said he was always a little transparent but moved with his own will, not hers. Tell me your poem.'

> When I was but thirteen or so
> I went into a golden land,
> Chimborazo, Cotopaxi
> Took me by the hand.

The Djinn in the Nightingale's Eye

My father died, my brother too,
They passed like fleeting dreams,
I stood where Popocatapetl
In the sunlight gleams.

I dimly heard the Master's voice,
And boys' far-off at play,
Chimborazo, Cotopaxi
Had stolen me away.

I walked in a great golden dream
To and fro from school –
Shining Popocatapetl
The dusty streets did rule.

I walked home with a gold dark boy
And never a word I'd say
Chimborazo, Cotopaxi
Had taken my speech away:

I gazed entranced upon his face
Fairer than any flower –
O shining Popocatapetl
It was thy magic hour:

The houses, people, traffic seemed
Thin fading dreams by day,

Chimborazo, Cotopaxi
They had stolen my soul away.

'I love that poem,' said Dr Perholt. 'It has two things: names and the golden boy. The names are not the names of the boy, they are the romance of language, and *he* is the romance of language – he is more real than – reality – as the goddess of Ephesus is more real than I am – '

'And I am here,' said the djinn.

'Indeed,' said Dr Perholt. 'Incontrovertibly.'

There was a silence. The djinn returned to the topic of Dr Perholt's husband, her children, her house, her parents, all of which she answered without – in her mind or his – investing any of these now truly insignificant people with any life or colour. My husband went to Majorca with Emmeline Porter, she said to the djinn, and decided not to come back, and I was glad. The djinn asked about the complexion of Mr Perholt and the nature of the beauty of Emmeline Porter and received null and unsatisfactory answers. They are wax images, your people, said the djinn indignantly.

'I do not want to think about them.'

'That is apparent. Tell me something about

yourself – something you have never told anyone –
something you have never trusted to any lover in
the depth of any night, to any friend, in the warmth
of a long evening. Something you have kept for
me.'

And the image sprang in her mind, and she rejected it as insignificant.

'Tell me,' said the djinn.

'It is insignificant.'

'Tell me.'

'Once, I was a bridesmaid. To a good friend
from my college who wanted a white wedding,
with veils and flowers and organ music, though she
was happily settled with her man already, they
slept together, she said she was blissfully happy,
and I believe she was. At college, she seemed very
poised and formidable – a woman of power, a
woman of sexual experience, which was unusual in
my day – '

'Women have always found ways – '

'Don't sound like the *Arabian Nights*. I am telling
you something. She was full of bodily grace, and
capable of being happy, which most of us
were not, it was fashionable to be disturbed and

anguished, for young women in those days – probably young men too. We were a generation when
there was something shameful about being an un-
married woman, a spinster – though we were all
clever, like Zefir, my friends and I, we all had this
greed for knowledge – we were scholars – '

'Zefir would have been happy as a teacher of
philosophy, it is true,' said the djinn. 'Neither of
us could quite think what she could be – in those
days – '

'And my friend – whom I shall call Susannah, it
wasn't her name, but I can't go on without one –
my friend had always seemed to me to come from
somewhere rather grand, a beautiful house with
beautiful things. But when I arrived for the wedding her house was much like mine, small, like a
box, in a row of similar houses, and there was a
settee, there was a three-piece suite in moquette – '

'A three-piece suite in moquette?' enquired the
djinn. 'What horrid thing is this to make you frown
so?'

'I knew it was no good telling you anything out
of my world. It is too big for those rooms, it is too
heavy, it *weighs everything down*, it is chairs and a

sofa that sat on a beige carpet with splashy flowers on – '

'A sofa – ' said the djinn, recognising a word. 'A carpet.'

'You don't know what I'm talking about. I should never have started on this. All English stories get bogged down in whether or not the furniture is socially and aesthetically acceptable. This wasn't. That is, I thought so then. Now I find everything interesting, because I live my own life.'

'Do not heat yourself. You did not like the house. The house was small and the three-piece suite in moquette was big, I comprehend. Tell me about the marriage. The story is presumably about the marriage and not about the chairs and sofa.'

'Not really. The marriage went off beautifully. She had a lovely dress, like a princess out of a story – those were the days of the princess-line in dresses – I had a princess-line dress too, in shot taffeta, turquoise and silver, with a heart-shaped neck, and she was wearing several net skirts, and over those silk, and over that white lace – and a *mass* of veiling – and real flowers in her hair – little rosebuds –

there wasn't room for all those billows of wonderful stuff in her tiny bedroom. She had a bedside lamp with Peter Rabbit eating a carrot. And all this shimmering silk and stuff. On the day, she looked so lovely, out of another world. I had a big hat with a brim, it suited me. You can imagine the dresses, I expect, but you can't imagine the house, the place.'

'If you say I cannot,' replied the djinn, obligingly. 'Why do you tell me this tale? I cannot believe this is what you have not told.'

'The night before the wedding,' said Gillian Perholt, 'we bathed together, in her parents' little bathroom. It had tiles with fishes with trailing fins and big soulful cartoon eyes – '

'Cartoon?'

'Disney. It doesn't matter. *Comic* eyes.'

'Comic tiles?'

'It doesn't matter. We didn't share the bath, but we washed together.'

'And – ' said the djinn. 'She made love to you.'

'No,' said Dr Perholt. 'She didn't. I saw myself. First in the mirror, and then I looked down at myself. And then I looked across at her – she was

pearly-white and I was more golden. And she was
soft and sweet – '

'And you were not?'

'I was perfect. Just at that moment, just at the
very end of being a girl, and before I was a woman,
really, I was perfect.'

She remembered seeing her own small, beautifully rising breasts, her warm, flat, tight belly, her
long slender legs and ankles, her waist – her waist –

'She said, "Some man is going to go mad with
desire for you",' said Gillian Perholt. 'And I was all
proud inside my skin, as never before or since. All
golden.' She thought. 'Two girls in a suburban
bathroom,' she said, in an English deprecating
voice.

The djinn said, 'But when I changed you, that
was not what you became. You are very nice now,
very acceptable, very desirable now, but not perfect.'

'It was terrifying. I was terrified. It was like – '
she found a completely unexpected phrase – 'like
having a weapon, a sharp sword, I couldn't handle.'

'Ah yes,' said the djinn. 'Terrible as an army with
banners.'

'But it didn't belong to me. I was tempted to – to love it – myself. It was lovely. But unreal. I mean, it was *there*, it was real enough, but I knew in my head it wouldn't stay – something would happen to it. I owed it – ' she went on, searching for feelings she had never interrogated – 'I owed it – some sort of adequate act. And I wasn't going to live up to it.' She caught her breath on a sigh. 'I am a creature of the mind, not the body, Djinn. I can look after my mind. I took care of that, despite everything.'

'Is that the end of the story?' said the djinn after another silence. 'Your stories are strange, glancing things. They peter out, they have no shape.'

'It is what my culture likes, or liked. But no, it is not the end. There is a little bit more. In the morning Susannah's father brought my breakfast in bed. A boiled egg in a woolly cosy, a little silver-plated pot of tea, in a cosy knitted to look like a cottage, toast in a toast-rack, butter in a butter-dish, all on a little tray with unfolding legs, like the trays old ladies have in Homes.'

'You didn't like the – the whatever was on the teapot? Your aesthetic sense, which is so violent, was in revolt again?'

'He suddenly leaned forwards and pulled my nightdress off my shoulders. He put his hands round my perfect breasts,' said Dr Perholt who was fifty-five and now looked thirty-two, 'and he put his sad face down between them – he had glasses, they were all steamed up and knocked sideways, he had a little bristly moustache that crept over my flesh like a centipede, he *snuffled* amongst my breasts, and all he said was "I can't bear it" and he rubbed his body against my counterpane – I only half-understood, the counterpane was artificial silk, eau-de-nil colour – he snuffled and jerked and twisted my breasts in his hands – and then he un-folded the little legs of the tray and put it over my legs and went away – to give away his daughter, which he did with great dignity and charm. And I felt sick, and felt my body was to blame. As though out of *that*,' she said lucidly, 'was spun snuffling and sweat and three-piece suites and artificial silk and teacosies – '

'And that is the end of the story?' said the djinn.

'That is where a storyteller would end it, in my country.'

'Odd. And you met *me* and asked for the body of a thirty-two-year-old woman.'

'I didn't. I asked for it to be as it was when I last *liked* it. I didn't like it then. I half-worshipped it, but it scared me – This is *my* body, I find it pleasant, I don't mind looking at it – '

'Like the potter who puts a deliberate flaw in the perfect pot.'

'Maybe. If having lived a little is a flaw. Which it is. That girl's ignorance was a burden to her.'

'Do you know now what other things you will wish for?'

'Ah, you are anxious to be free.'

'On the contrary, I am comfortable, I am curious, I have all the time in the world.'

'And I have everything I wish for, at present. I have been thinking about the story of the Queen of Sheba and what the answer might be to the question of what all women desire. I shall tell you the story of the Ethiopian woman whom I saw on the television box.'

'I am all ears,' said the djinn, extending himself on the bedspread and shrinking himself a little, in order to be able to accommodate himself at full length. 'Tell me, this box, you can turn it to spy anywhere you desire in the world, you can see Manaus or Khartoum as you please?'

'Not exactly, though partly. For instance the tennis was coming live – we call it "live" when we see it simultaneously with its happening – from Monte Carlo. But also we can make images – stories – which we can replay to ourselves. The Ethiopian woman was part of a story – a film – made for the Save the Children Fund – which is a charitable body – which had given some food to a village in Ethiopia where there had been drought and famine, food specifically to give to the children, to keep them alive through the winter. And when they brought the food, they filmed the people of the village, the head men and the elders, the children playing, and then they came back, the research workers came back, half a year later, to see the children and weigh them, to see how the food they had given had helped them.'

'Ethiopia is a fierce country of fierce people,' said the djinn. 'Beautiful and terrible. What did you see in your box?'

'The aid workers were very angry – distressed

and angry. The head man had promised to give the food only to the families with the small children the project was helping and studying – "project" is – '

'I know. I have known projectors in my time.'

'But the head man had not done as he was asked. It was against his beliefs to feed some families and not others, and it was against everyone's beliefs to feed small children and not grown men, who could work in the fields, if anything could be grown there. So the food had been shared out too sparsely – and everyone was thinner – and some of the children were dead – many, I think – and others were very ill because the food had not been given to them.

'And the workers – the relief workers – the charitable people from America and Europe – were angry and upset – and the cameramen (the people who make the films) went out into the fields with the men who had had the food, and had sowed their crops in hope of rain – and had even had a little rain – and the men lifted the seedlings and showed the cameramen and the officials that the roots had been eaten away by a plague of sawfly, and there would be no harvest. And those men, standing in those

246

fields, holding those dying, stunted seedlings, were in complete despair. They had no hope and no idea what to do. We had seen the starving in great gatherings on our boxes, you must understand – we knew where they were heading, and had sent the food because we were moved because of what we had seen.

'And then, the cameras went into a little hut, and there in the dark were four generations of women, the grandmother, the mother and the young girl with her baby. The mother was stirring something in a pot over a fire – it looked like a watery soup – with a wooden stick – and the grandmother was sitting on a kind of bed against the wall, where the hut roof – which seemed conical – met it. They were terribly thin, but they weren't dying – they hadn't given up yet, they hadn't got those eyes looking out at nothing, or those slack muscles just waiting. They were beautiful people still, people with long faces and extraordinary cheek-bones, and a kind of dignity in their movement – or what westerners like me read as dignity, they are upright, they carry their heads up –

'And they interviewed the old woman. I remember it partly because of her beauty, and partly because of the skill of the cameraman – or woman – she was angular but not awkward, and she had one long arm at an angle over her head, and her legs extended on this bench – and the photographer had made them squared, as it were *framed* in her own limbs – she spoke out of an enclosure made by her own body, and her eyes were dark holes and her face was long, long. She made the edges of the box out of her body. They wrote in English letters across the screen a translation of what she was saying. She said there was no food, no food any more and the little girl would starve, and there would be no milk, there would be no more food. And then she said "It is because I am a woman, I cannot get out of here, I must sit here and wait for my fate, if only I were not a woman I could go out and do something – " all in a monotone. With the men stomping about in the furrows outside kicking up dry dust and stunted seedlings in perfect despair.

'I don't know why I tell you this. I will tell you something else. I was told to wish on a pillar in Haghia Sophia – and before I could stop myself – it was – not a good pillar – I wished what I used to wish as a child.'

'You wished you were not a woman.'

'There were three veiled women laughing at me, pushing my hand into that hole.

'I thought, perhaps, that was what the Queen of Sheba told Solomon that all women desired.'

The genie smiled.

'It was not. That was not what she told him. Not exactly.'

'Will you tell me what she told him?'

'If you wish me to.'

'I wish – Oh, no. No, that isn't what I wish.'

Gillian Perholt looked at the djinn on her bed. The evening had come, whilst they sat there, telling each other stories. A kind of light played over his green-gold skin, and a kind of glitter, like the glitter from the Byzantine mosaics, where a stone here or there will be set at a slight angle to catch the light. His plumes rose and fell as though they were breathing, silver and crimson, chrysanthemum-bronze and lemon, sapphire-blue and emerald. There was an edge of sulphur to his scent, and sandalwood, she thought, and something bitter –

myrrh, she wondered, having never smelt myrrh,
but remembering the king in the Christmas carol

> Myrrh is mine, its bitter perfume
> Breathes a life of gathering gloom,
> Sorrowing, sighing, bleeding, dying
> Sealed in a stone-cold tomb.

The outsides of his thighs were greener and the in-
sides softer and more golden. He had pulled down
his tunic, not entirely adequately: she could see his
sex coiled like a folded snake and stirring.

'I wish,' said Dr Perholt to the djinn, 'I wish you
would love me.'

'You honour me,' said the djinn, 'and maybe you
have wasted your wish, for it may well be that love
would have happened anyway, since we are together, and sharing our life stories, as lovers do.'

'Love,' said Gillian Perholt, 'requires generos-
ity. I found I was jealous of Zefir and I have never
been jealous of anyone. I wanted – it was more that
I wanted to give *you* something – to give you my
wish – ' she said, incoherently. The great eyes,
stones of many greens, considered her and the
carved mouth lifted in a smile.

'You give and you bind,' said the djinn, 'like all lovers. You give yourself, which is brave, and which I think you have never done before – and I find you eminently lovable. Come.'

And without moving a muscle Dr Perholt found herself naked on the bed, in the arms of the djinn.

Of their love-making she retained a memory at once precise, mapped on to every nerve-ending, and indescribable. There was, in any case, no one to whom she could have wished to describe the love-making of a djinn. All love-making is shape-shifting – the male expands like a tree, like a pillar, the female has intimations of infinity in the spaces which narrow inside her. But the djinn could pro-long everything, both in space and in time, so that Gillian seemed to swim across his body forever like a dolphin in an endless green sea, so that she be-came arching tunnels under mountains through which he pierced and rushed, or caverns in which he lay curled like dragons. He could become a con-centrated point of delight at the pleasure-points of her arched and delighted body; he could travel her like some wonderful butterfly, brushing her here and there with a hot, dry, almost burning kiss, and then become again a folding landscape in which she rested and was lost, lost herself for him to find her again, holding her in the palm of his great hand, contracting himself with a sigh and holding her breast to breast, belly to belly, male to female. His sweat was like a smoke and he murmured like a cloud of bees in many languages – she felt her skin was on fire and was not consumed, and tried once to tell him about Marvell's lovers who had not 'world enough and time' but could only murmur one couplet in the green cave of his ear. 'My veget-able love should grow/Vaster than empires and more slow.' Which the djinn smilingly repeated, using the rhythm for a particularly delectable movement of his body.

And afterwards she slept. And woke alone in her pretty nightdress, amongst her pillows. And rose sadly and went to the bathroom, where the çesm-i bülbül bottle still stood, with her own finger-traces on its moist sides. She touched it sadly, running her fingers down the spirals of white – I have had a dream, she thought – and there was the djinn, bent into the bathroom like the Ethiopian woman in the television box, making an effort to adjust his size.

'I thought – '

'I know. But as you see, I am here.'

'Will you come to England with me?'

'I must, if you ask me. But also I should like to do that, I should like to see how things are now, in the world, I should like to see where you live, though you cannot describe it as interesting.'

'It will be, if you are there.'

But she was afraid.

And they went back to England, the narratologist, the glass bottle, and the djinn; they went back by British Airways, with the bottle cushioned in bubble plastic in a bag at Gillian Perholt's feet.

And when they got back, Dr Perholt found that the wish she had made before Artemis between the two Leylas was also granted: there was a letter asking her to give the keynote paper in Toronto in the fall, and offering her a Club-class fare and a stay in the Xanadu Hotel, which did indeed have a swimming-pool, a blue pool under a glass dome, sixty-four floors above Lake Superior's shores.

And it was cold and clear in Toronto, and Dr Perholt settled herself into the hotel room, which was
tastefully done in warm colours for cold winters, in
chestnuts, browns and ambers, with touches of
flame. Hotel rooms have often the illusory presence of a magician's stage set – their walls are bare
concrete boxes, covered with whipped-up white
plaster, like icing on a cake, and then the soft things
are hung from screwed-in poles and hooks, damask
and voile, gilt-edged mirror and branching cande-
labra, to give the illusion of richness. But all could
be swept away in a twinkling and replaced by quite
other colours and textures – chrome for brass,
purple for amber, white-spotted muslin for gold
damask, and this spick-and-span temporariness is
part of the charm. Dr Perholt unpacked the nightingale's-eye bottle and opened the stopper, and the
djinn came out, human-size, and waved his wing-
cloak to uncramp it. He then shot out of the window to look at the lake and the city, and returned,
saying that she must come with him over the water,
which was huge and cold, and that the sky, the
atmosphere, was so full of rushing faces and figures
that he had had to thread his way between them.

The filling of the air-waves with politicians and pop-stars, TV evangelists and vacuum cleaners, moving forests and travelling deserts, pornographic bottoms and mouths and navels, purple felt dinosaurs and insane white puppies – all this had deeply saddened the djinn, almost to the point of depression. He was like someone who had had the habit of riding alone across deserts on a camel, or rushing off across savannah on an Arab horse, and now found himself negotiating an endless traffic-jam of film-stars, tennis-players and comedians, amongst the Boeings circling to find landing-slots. The Koran and the Old Testament, he told Dr Perholt, forbade the making of graven images, and whilst these were not graven, they were images, and he felt they were infestations. The atmosphere, he told her, had always been full of unseen beings – unseen by her kind – and still was. But it now needed to be negotiated. It is as bad, said the djinn, in the upper air as in bottles. I cannot spread my wings.

'And if you were entirely free,' said Dr Perholt, 'where would you go?'

'There is a land of fire – where my kind play in the flames –'

They looked at each other.

'But I do not want to go,' said the djinn gently. 'I love you, and I have all the time in the world. And all this chatter and all these flying faces, they are also interesting. I learn many languages. I speak many tongues. Listen.'

And he made a perfect imitation of Donald Duck, followed by a perfect imitation of Chancellor Kohl's orotund German, followed by the voices of the Muppets, followed by a surprising rendition of Kiri Te Kanawa which had Dr Perholt's neighbours banging on the partition wall.

The conference was in Toronto University, ivy-hung in Victorian Gothic. It was a prestigious conference, to use an adjective that at this precise moment is shifting its meaning from magical, from conjuring-tricks, to 'full of renown', 'respectable in the highest', 'most honourable'. The French narratologists were there, Todorov and Genette, and there were various orientalists too, on the watch for western sentiment and distortion. Gillian Per-holt's title was 'Wish-fulfilment and Narrative Fate: some aspects of wish-fulfilment as a narrative device'. She had sat up late writing it. She had never learned not to put her lectures together under pressure and at the last minute. It was not that she had not thought the subject-matter out in advance. She had. She had thought long and care-fully, with the çesm-i bülbül bottle set before her like a holy image, with its blue and white stripes enfolding each other and circling and diminishing to its mouth. She had looked at her own strong pretty newish fingers travelling across the page, and flexed the comfortable stomach-muscles. She had tried to be precise. Yet she felt, as she stood up to speak, that her subject had taken a great twist in her hands, like a magic flounder trying to return to the sea, like a divining-rod pointing with its own energy into the earth, like a conducting-rod shiver-ing with the electrical forces in the air.

As usual, she had tried to incorporate the telling of a story, and it was this story that had somehow twisted the paper away from its subject. It would be tedious to recount all her arguments. Their tenor can be guessed from their beginning.

'Characters in fairy-tales,' said Gillian, 'are subject to Fate and enact their fates. Characteristically they attempt to change this fate by magical intervention in its workings, and characteristically too, such magical intervention only reinforces the control of the Fate which waited for them, which is perhaps simply the fact that they are mortal and return to dust. The most clear and absolute version of this narrative form is the story of the appointment in Samarra – of the man who meets Death, who tells him that he is coming for him that evening, and flees to Samarra to avoid him. And Death remarks to an acquaintance that their first meeting was odd "since I was to meet him in Samarra tonight."

'Novels in recent time, have been about choice and motivation. Something of the ineluctable consequentiality of Samarra still clings to Raskolnikov's "free" act of murder, for it calls down a wholly predictable and conventional vengeance. In the case of George Eliot's Lydgate, on the other hand, we do not feel that the "spots of

commonness" in his nature are instruments of inevitable fate in the same way: it was possible for
him *not* to choose to marry Rosamund and destroy
his fortune and his ambition. We feel that when
Proust decides to diagnose sexual inversion in *all*
his characters he is substituting the novelist's
desires for the Fate of the real world; and yet that
when Swann wastes years of his life for a woman
who was not even his type, he made a choice, in
time, that was possible but not inevitable.

'The emotion we feel in fairy-tales when the
characters are granted their wishes is a strange one.
We feel the possible leap of freedom – I can have
what I want – and the perverse certainty that this
will change nothing; that Fate is fixed.

'I should like to tell you a story told to me by a
friend I met in Turkey – where stories are introduced *bir var mis, bir yok mis,* perhaps it
happened, perhaps it didn't, and have paradox as
their inception.'

She looked up, and there, sitting next to the
handsome figure of Todorov, was a heavy-headed
person in a sheepskin jacket, with a huge head of

white hair. This person had not been there before, and the white mane had the look of an extravagant toupée, which, with blue-tinted glasses, gave the newcomer a look of being cruelly in disguise. Gillian thought she recognised the lift of his upper lip, which immediately changed shape under her eyes as soon as she had this thought, becoming defiantly thin and pursed. She could not see into the eyes: when she tried, the glasses became almost sapphire in their rebarbative glitter.

'In the days when camels flew from roof to roof,' she began, 'and fish roosted in cherry trees, and peacocks were as huge as haystacks, there was a fisherman who had nothing, and who moreover had no luck fishing, for he caught nothing, though he cast his net over and over in a great lake full of weeds and good water. And he said, one more cast, and if that brings up nothing, I shall give up this métier, which is starving me, and take to begging at the roadside. So he cast, and his net was heavy, and he pulled in something wet and rolling and malodorous, which turned out to be a dead ape. So he said to himself, that is not nothing, nevertheless, and he dug a hole in the sand and buried the ape, and cast his net again, for a second last time. And this time too, it was full, and this time it struggled under the water, with a life of its own. So he pulled it up, full of hope, and what he had caught was a second ape, a moribund toothless ape, with great sores and scabs on its body, and a smell almost as disagreeable as its predecessor. Well, said the fisherman, I could tidy up this beast, and sell him to some street musician. He did not like the prospect. The ape then said to him – If you let me go, and cast again, you will catch my brother. And if you do not listen to his pleas, or make any more casts, he will stay with you and grant you anything you may wish for. There is a snag, of course, there is always a snag, but I am not about to tell you what it is.

'This limited honesty appealed to the fisherman, who disentangled the thin ape without much more ado, and cast again, and the net struggled away with satisfactory violence and it took all his force to bring it to shore. And indeed it contained an ape, a very large, glossy, *gleaming* ape, with, so my friend particularly told me, a most beautiful bottom, a mixture of very bright subtle blue, and a hot rose-colour, suffused with poppy-coloured veins.'

She looked at the sapphire-coloured dark glasses to see if she had done well and their owner nodded tersely.

'So the new ape said that if the fisherman would release him, and cast again, he would draw up a huge treasure, and a palace, and a company of slaves, and never want again. But the fisherman remembered the saying of the thin ape, and said to the new one "I wish for a new house, on the shore of this lake, and I wish for a camel, and I wish for a feast – of moderate proportions – to be ready-cooked in this house."

'And immediately all these things appeared, and the fisherman offered a share of the delicious feast to the two apes, and they accepted.

'And he was a fisherman who had heard a great many tales in his time, and had an analytic bent, and he thought he understood that the danger of wishes lay in being overweening or hasty. He had no wish to find himself in a world where everything was made of gold and was quite inedible, and he had a strong intuition that the perpetual company of houris or the perpetual imbibing of sherbet and sparkling wine would be curiously wearisome.

So he wished quietly for this and that: a shop full of tiles to sell and an assistant who understood them and was honest, a garden full of cedars and fountains, a little house with a servant-girl for his old mother, and finally a little wife, such as his mother would have chosen for him, who was not to be beautiful as the sun and moon but kind and comfortable and loving. And so he went on, very peacefully, creating a world much more like the peaceful world of "happy-ever-after" outside tales than the hectic one of the wishes granted by Grimm's flounder, or even Aladdin's djinn. And no one noticed his good fortune, much, and no one envied him or tried to steal it, since he was so discreet. And if he fell ill, or his little wife fell ill, he wished the illness away, and if someone spoke harshly to him he wished to forget it, and forgot.

'And the snag, you ask?

'This was the snag. He began to notice, slowly at first, and then quicker and quicker, that every time he made a wish, the great gleaming ape became a little smaller. At first just a centimetre there, and a centimetre here, and then more and more, so that he had to be raised on many cushions to eat his meals, and finally became so small that he sat on a little stool on top of the dining-table and toyed with a tiny junket in a salt-cellar. The thin ape had long gone his way, and returned again from time to time, now looking quite restored, in an ordinary sort of hairy way, with an ordinary blue bottom, nothing to be excited about. And the fisherman said to the thin ape.

'"What will happen if I wish him larger again?"'

'"I cannot say," said the ape. "That is to say, I won't say."'

'And at night the fisherman heard the two apes talking. The thin one held the shining one in his hand and said sadly.

'"It goes ill with you, my poor brother. You will vanish away soon; there will be nothing left of you. It is sad to see you in this state."'

'"It is my Fate," said the once-larger ape. "It is my Fate to lose power and to diminish. One day I shall be so small, I shall be invisible, and the man will not be able to see me any more to make any more wishes, and there I shall be, a slave-ape the size of a pepper-grain or a grain of sand."'

'"We all come to dust," said the thin ape sententiously.

'"But not with this terrible speed," said the wishing-ape. "I do my best, but still I am used and used. It is hard. I wish I were dead but none of my own wishes may be granted. Oh, it is hard, it is hard, it is hard."

'"And at this, the fisherman, who was a good man, rose out of his bed and went into the room where the two apes were talking, and said,

'"I could not help hearing you and my heart is wrung for you. What can I do, O apes, to help you?"

'And they looked at him sullenly and would not answer.

'"I wish," said the fisherman then, "that you would take the next wish, if that is possible, and wish for your heart's desire."

'And then he waited to see what would happen.

'And both apes vanished as if they had never been.

'But the house, and the wife, and the prosperous business did not vanish. And the fisherman continued to live as well as he could – though subject

now to ordinary human ailments with the rest of us
– until the day he died.'

'In fairy-tales,' said Gillian, 'those wishes that are
granted and are not malign, or twisted towards
destruction, tend to lead to a condition of beautiful
stasis, more like a work of art than the drama of
Fate. It is as though the fortunate had stepped off
the hard road into an unchanging landscape where
it is always spring and no winds blow. Aladdin's
genie gives him a beautiful palace, and as long as
this palace is subject to Fate, various magicians
move it violently around the landscape, build it up
and cause it to vanish. But at the end, it goes into
stasis: into the pseudo-eternity of happy-ever-
after. When we imagine happy-ever-after we
imagine works of art: a family photograph on a
sunny day, a Gainsborough lady and her children
in an English meadow under a tree, an enchanted
castle in a snowstorm of feathers in a glass dome. It
was Oscar Wilde's genius to make the human
being and the work of art change places. Dorian
Gray smiles unchangingly in his eternal youth and
his portrait undergoes his Fate, which is a terrible

one, a fate of accelerating deterioration. The tale of Dorian Gray and also Balzac's tale of *La Peau de Chagrin*, the diminishing piece of wild-ass's skin that for a time keeps Fate at bay, are related to other tales of the desire for eternal youth. Indeed we have methods now of granting a kind of false stasis, we have prostheses and growth hormone, we have plastic surgery and implanted hair, we can make humans into works of some kind of art or artifice. The grim and gallant fixed stares of Joan Collins and Barbara Cartland are icons of our wish for this kind of eternity.

'The tale of the apes, I think, relates to the observations of Sigmund Freud on the goal of all life. Freud was, whatever else he was, the great student of our desire, our will to live happily ever after. He studied our wishes, our fulfilment of our wishes, in the narrative of our dreams. He believed we rearranged our stories in our dream-life to give ourselves happy endings, each according to his or her secret needs. (He claimed not to know what women really wanted, and this ignorance colours and changes his stories.) Then, in the repeated death-dreams of the soldiers of the First World

War he discovered a narrative that contradicted this desire for happiness, for wish-fulfilment. He discovered, he thought, a desire for annihilation. He rethought the whole history of organic life under the sun, and came to the conclusion that what he called the 'organic instincts' were essentially *conservative* – that they reacted to stimuli by adapting in order to preserve, as far as possible, their original state. 'It would be in contradiction to the conservative nature of the instincts,' said Freud, 'if the goal of life were a state of things which had never been attained.' No, he said, what we desire must necessarily be an *old* state of things. Organisms strive, circuitously, to return to the inorganic – the dust, the stone, the earth – from which they came. *"The aim of all life is death,"* said Freud, telling his creation story in which the creation strives to return to the state before life was breathed into it, in which the shrinking of the peau de chagrin, the diminishing of the ape, is not the terrible concomitant of the life-force, but its secret desire.'

This was not all she said, but this was the second

point at which she caught a flash of the sapphire glasses.

There were many questions, and Gillian's paper was judged a success, if somewhat confused.

Back in her hotel bedroom that night she confronted the djinn.

'You made my paper incoherent,' she said. 'It was a paper about fate and death and desire, and you introduced the freedom of wishing-apes.'

'I do not see what is incoherent,' said the djinn. 'Entropy rules us all. Power gets less, whether it derives from the magic arts or is made by nerves and muscle.'

Gillian said, 'I am ready now to make my third wish.'

'I am all ears,' said the djinn, momentarily expanding those organs to the size of elephants' ears. 'Do not look doleful, Djil-yan, it may not happen.'

'And where did you learn that catch-phrase? Never mind. I shall almost believe you are trying to prevent my wish.'

'No, no. I am your slave.'

'I wish,' said Gillian, 'I wish you could have whatever you wish for – that this last wish may be your wish.'

And she waited for the sound of thunder, or worse, the silence of absence. But what she heard was the sound of breaking glass. And she saw her bottle, the nightingale's-eye bottle, which stood on a glass sheet on the dressing-table, dissolve like tears, not into sharp splinters, but into a conical heap of tiny cobalt blue glass marbles, each with a white spiral coiled inside it.

'Thank you,' said the djinn.

'Will you go?' asked the narratologist.

'Soon,' said the djinn. 'Not now, not immediately. You wished also, remember, that I would love you, and so I do. I shall give you something to remember me by – until I return – which, from time to time, I shall do – '

'If you remember to return in my life-time,' said Gillian Perholt.

'If I do,' said the djinn, whose body now seemed to be clothed in a garment of liquid blue flame.

That night he made love to her, so beautifully that she wondered simultaneously how she could ever have let him go, and how she could ever have dared to keep such a being in Primrose Hill, or in hotel bedrooms in Istanbul or Toronto.

And the next morning he appeared in jeans and a sheepskin jacket, and said they were going out together, to find a gift. This time his hair – still fairly improbable – was a mass of dreadlocks, and his skin inclined to the Ethiopian.

In a small shop, in a side-street, he showed her the most beautiful collection of modern weights she had ever seen. It is a modern Canadian art; they have artists who can trap a meshed and rolling geometrical sea, only visible at certain angles, and when visible glitters transparently with a rainbow of particles dusted with gold; they have artists who can enclose a red and blue flame forever in a cool glass sphere, or a dizzy cone of cobalt and emerald, reaching to infinity and meeting its own reflection. Glass is made of dust, of silica, of the sand of the desert, melted in a fiery furnace and blown into its solid form by human breath. It is fire and ice, it is liquid and solid, it is there and not there.

The djinn put into Dr Perholt's hands a huge,

slightly domed sphere inside which were suspended like commas, like fishing-hooks, like fireworks, like sleeping embryos, like spurts of coloured smoke, like uncurling serpents, a host of coloured ribbons of glass amongst a host of breathed bubbles. They were all colours – gold and yellow, bright blue and dark blue, a delectable clear pink, a crimson, a velvet green, a whole host of busy movement. 'Like rushing seed,' said the djinn poetically. 'Full of forever possibilities. And impossibilities, of course. It is a work of art, a great work of craft, it is a joyful thing, you like it?'

'Oh, yes,' said Dr Perholt. 'I have never seen so many colours in one.'

'It is called "The Dance of the Elements",' said the djinn. 'I think that it is not your sort of title, but it suits it, I think. No?'

'Yes,' said Dr Perholt, who was sorrowful and yet full of a sense of things being as they should be.

The djinn watched the wrapping of the weight in shocking-pink tissue, and paid for it with a rainbow-coloured credit card with a hologram of the Venus de Milo, which caused an almost excessive fizzing amongst the terminals in the card machine.

On the pavement he said,

'Good bye. For the present.'

'"Now to the elements," ' said Dr Perholt, ' "Be free and fare thou well." '

She had thought of saying that some day, ever since she had first seen his monstrous foot from her bathroom door. She stood there, holding her glass weight. And the djinn kissed her hand, and vanished towards Lake Superior like a huge cloud of bees, leaving behind on the pavement a sheep-skin jacket that shrank slowly, to childsize, to doll size, to matchbox size, to a few fizzing atoms, and was gone. He left also a moving heap of dread-locks, like some strange hedgehog, which stirred a little, ran along a few feet, and vanished down a drain.

And did she ever see him again, you may ask? Or that may not be the question uppermost in your mind, but it is the only one to which you get an answer.

Two years ago, still looking thirty-five and com-fortable, she was walking along Madison Avenue in New York, during a stop on the way to a narratological gathering in British Columbia, when she saw a shop window full of paperweights. These were not the work of artists like the Toronto artists who play with pure colour and texture, ribbons and threads and veils, stains and illusory movement. These were pure, old-fashioned, skilful representations: millefiori, lattice work, crowns, canes, containing roses and violets, lizards and butterflies. Dr Perholt went in, her eyes gleaming like the glass, and there in the dark shop were two elderly and charming men, happy men in a cavern bright with jewels, who for half an hour and with exquisite patience fetched out for Dr Perholt sphere after sphere from the glass shelves in which they were reflected, and admired with her basket-work of fine white containing cornflower-blue posies, multi-coloured cushions of geometric flowers, lovely as Paradise must have been in its glistening newness, bright with a brightness that would never fade, never come out into the dull air from its brilliant element.

Oh *glass*, said Dr Perholt to the two gentlemen, it is not possible, it is only a solid metaphor, it is a medium for seeing and a thing seen at once. It is what art is, said Dr Perholt to the two men, as they moved the balls of light, red, blue, green, on the visible and the invisible shelves.

'I like the geometrically patterned flowers best,' said Dr Perholt. 'More than the ones that aim at realism, at looking real, don't you agree?'

'On the whole,' said one of the two. 'On the whole, the whole effect is better with the patterning, with the geometry of the glass and the geometry of the canes. But have you seen these? These are American.'

And he gave her a weight in which a small snake lay curled on a watery surface of floating duckweed – a snake with a glass thread of a flickering tongue and an almost microscopic red-brown eye in its watchful but relaxed olive head. And he gave her a weight in which, in the solidity of the glass as though it were the deep water of a well, floated a flower, a flower with a rosy lip and a white hood, a green stem, long leaves trailing in the water, and a root specked and stained with its brown juices and the earth it had come from, a root trailing fine hair-roots and threads and tendrils into the glassy medium. It was perfect because the illusion was near-perfect, and the attention to the living original had been so perfect that the undying artificial flower also seemed perfect. And Gillian thought of Gilgamesh, and the lost flower, and the snake. Here they were side by side, held in suspension.

She turned the weight over, and put it down, for its price was prohibitive.

She noticed, almost abstractedly, that there was a new dark age-stain on the back of the hand that held the weight. It was a pretty soft dried-leaf colour.

'I wish – ' she said to the man behind the glass cage of shelves.

'You would like the flower,' said a voice behind her. 'And the snake with it, why not? I will give them to you.'

And there he was behind her, this time in a dark overcoat and a white scarf, with a rather large wide-brimmed black velvet hat, and the sapphire glasses.

'What a nice surprise to see you again, sir,' said

the shopowner, holding out his hand for the rainbow credit card with the Venus de Milo. 'Always unexpected, always welcome, most welcome.'

And Dr Perholt walked out into Madison Avenue with a gold-dark man and two weights, a snake and a flower. There are things in the earth, things made with hands and beings not made with hands that live a life different from ours, that live longer than we do, and cross our lives in stories, in dreams, at certain times when we are floating redundant. And Gillian Perholt was happy, for she had moved back into their world, or at least had access to it, as she had had as a child. She said to the djinn,

'Will you stay?'

And he said, 'No. But I shall probably return again.'

And she said, 'If you remember to return in my life-time.'

'If I do,' said the djinn.

Acknowledgements

I am grateful to Cevat Çapan for help with things Turkish, my first introduction to çesm-i bülbül, and information about Cins, and I am grateful to Abdulrazak Gurnah who first drew my attention to the oddity of the third djinn in the story of Prince Camaralzaman. I am also generally grateful to Peter Carraciolo, whose enthusiasm for *The Arabian Nights* is infectious. Robert Irwin's splendid *The Arabian Nights: A Companion* came out whilst I was writing 'The Djinn in the Nightingale's Eye' and affected its ideas and its construction. Ruth Christie and Richard McKane who present the translation of the poems of Oktay Rifat in *Voices of Memory* (Rockingham Press, 1993) and the editors of *The Penguin Book of Turkish Verse* and of the recent *Modern Turkish Poetry* (Rockingham Press) must also be thanked. The British Council Literature Department has changed my vision of the world by sending me to many places. There was also a certain guide in the museum in Ankara . . .

'Dragons' Breath' was commissioned by Ineke Holzhaus and Ilonka Verdurment of the Sheherezade 2001 Foundation, and was read aloud in a shortened version during their project for Sarajevo. 'The Eldest Princess' was commissioned by Christine Park and Caroline Heaton for the Vintage collection of adult fairy stories, *Caught in a Story*. Christine had the idea that writers should write the fairy-tale of their own life, and I have always been worried about being the eldest of three sisters.

Jane Turner, as so often before, has given invaluable help with illustrations – we should make another book of her discoveries alone. Carmen Callil made the book beautiful and elegant and Jenny Uglow and Jonathan Burnham smoothed its progress.

I am grateful to Oxford University Press for permission to quote 'Romance' by W. J. Turner, *Selected Poems* (1939); and to Penguin Books Ltd for 'Göksu' by Faruk Nafiz Çamlibel and (in a slightly adapted version) 'Evening' by Ahmet Haşim, both from *The Penguin Book of Turkish Verse* (1978).